Chloe Anne

Force of Nature

Valerie Oblath (signature)

Valerie Oblath

cCc

THREE C'S PUBLISHING LLC

SAN MATEO, CA

Chloe Anne — Force of Nature
by Valerie Oblath

Three C's Publishing LLC
63 Bovet Rd., Suite 335
San Mateo, CA 94402

ISBN: 978-0-9800623-2-8

Library of Congress Control Number: 2007908055

Printed in the USA.

Dedication

The love we show our pets can't hold a candle to what they give to us in return. This book is for my "Three Cs"...

&

Ichabod,
Amigo,
Major,
Tina,
George,
Madam,
Prince...

Acknowledgments

My thanks—

To Vally Sharpe and Nancy Sayles Kaneshiro for their generous guidance to ensure *Chloe Anne* became a reality.

To Nate Garhart and Helga Hayse for answering my questions—trivial or not—with patience and perspective.

And a special thanks to Jean Ferrario and Rodney Anderson for their unwavering enthusiasm and support, and for loving my Chloe, Cinders and Cortes as their own.

Chloe Anne

Force of Nature

CHLOE: from the Greek; verdant and blooming

ANNE: from the Hebrew; gracious and merciful

PENNY: from the English; "with a web over her face"
(diminutive of Penelope)

Chapter One

* * * * *

I Have a Dream

In my youth, I had *real* dreams. Ah, to stalk a small mouse or savor a wren. To bring it home as a present to my owners, to sit proudly as I placed it at their feet. I was meant for glorious experiences, a life filled with celebrations, passion, and excitement. But dreams these were and only that. My existence was, in a word, *sans vie.*

Oh, the family I lived with was pleasant enough. I was petted routinely, fed two times a day—usually the garden variety of canned food—but food was food (or so I thought at the time). I had to stay indoors because my owners had declawed me. They must have had their reasons, but they never told me. Not a terribly pleasant experience, I might say. Even with drugs.

The upshot, though, is that my life became more than a little routine. I had no extracurricular activities. No exercise. No adventures. Only eating, sleeping, watching T.V., along with a daily poop. Perhaps that sounds a tad crass? Well, that's life. Or at least mine. In a word, pedestrian.

Come to think of it, so was my given name. "Penny." I mean, just take a look at this book's cover. Do *I* look like a "Penny" to you? See? A pedestrian choice. *Sans vie.*

So I'm living day-to-day. Is that all there is, I wondered? There must be more. I was meant for more! And then, just like Charleton Heston parting the Red Sea or George W. Bush getting an MBA from Harvard, a miracle happens. We're moving!!!

Yes, you heard it right. It was a Wednesday afternoon in early July, and I was reclining on the futon. Not the most comfortable of recliners but with the sun streaming through the blinds and a slight stir of warm air coming through the open window, my mind was in that hazy, fuzzy space between consciousness and sublime sleep. I could envision the warm, languid months of the remaining summer, my owners brushing me daily, ensuring all my winter's growth is removed. They say I'm a long-haired cat, with a domestic lineage. How gauche. I prefer soft and silky, gray and white tresses with pure white paws. My eyes are the purest of greens, like a meadow at the first of spring. Never plebian, only First Estate. But I digress...

In the background I heard bits and pieces of conversation. My owners had congregated at the dining room table. Their voices rose and fell, sounding excited. They didn't know I was near and for all intents and purposes, their chatter was not distracting me from my daydreams. Well, not until...

It will be so wonderful to be in a new and bigger place...lots of room...What shall we do with Penny?...The deposit's not too high...A garage. No more parking on the street....The

Humane Society....Someone will want her. She's such a good cat....I can't wait to pack.

I bolted upright...or a reasonable facsimile. After all, moving out of a reclining position *does* take effort. *What?* I wasn't going with them? Someone would *want* me? They were *discarding* me? No, no, no, this wouldn't do. I must have heard wrong. I was dreaming, in a fog.

Off the futon I jumped and made haste to the dining room. (How does one "make haste"? Is it broiled? Poached with a savory sauce perhaps?) My owners seemed oblivious to my presence....or maybe they didn't know I have ears. Well, I do and I hear just fine, thank you very much.

The landlord was fine with the 30 days, as long as we allow him to show the place at any time.

Will he call before coming in?

Yeah, no problem. I've told him that until we take Penny to the SPCA...

SPCA? SPCA? Sounded like a household disinfectant. What is SPCA?

...he should be careful not to let her out.

Let me out? Who in their right mind would let a declawed cat outside?

Then maybe we should take her sooner than later.

Might be a good idea. That way she won't be in the way when we pack.

I gasped (though to the humans I know...more of a cough).

Hi, girl. What's goin'on? A fur ball?

What had I done? They said I was a good girl. Then why didn't they want me with them? What had I done? Why couldn't I go with them?

So, why don't you check out the SPCA and find out what we have to do. Let's try to take care of this on a weekend. We'll have more time.

Penny, come over here. Time for a chin scratch.

Chin scratch? Don't touch me!!

Do you think she understands that we're giving her away?

Please, she's only a cat.

But....

You're always way too sentimental. She'll be fine. Everything's going to be fine.

6

Giving me away!?! No longer a gasp, cough, whatever you want to call it. I let forth with a howl.

Hey, dinner's not for an hour. C'mon, Penny, you can wait a little longer.

I raced to the bedroom, straight under the bed. My breathing was rapid, I was dizzy, my thoughts a blur. Is this what's called an anxiety attack? I tried to focus. I repeated my mantra, "I'm too beautiful for words. I'm too beautiful for words."

Time went by. No one came looking for me....not even a call to dinner. Slowly my heart rate returned to normal, my mind cleared. Putting my emotions aside, I tried to think logically. I needed to just sort things out. But not so slowly, the realization hit me: *I didn't have much choice.* Their words were as clear as can be. They were moving, and I wasn't part of the equation. I raised my head and squared my shoulders...very Scarlett O'Hara...and considered my options.

I'd always tried to see life as a water bowl half full so maybe it wouldn't be so bad. They did mention... what was it?...the Humane Society. I'd thought of myself as a society-sort of girl. And "humane" sounded as though it was an organization that was sort of caring. Maybe a group that did good things for others? I was sure I could fit in quite nicely. The name had a nice ring to it. Maybe other cats were members? Ones with breeding and style. A new group of friends. Perhaps they served an afternoon meal. Kind of a precursor to supper? With a little tuna? *This may not be so bad*, I thought. *The Humane Society.* I could see myself doing good works already. I would do just fine without my fair-weather owners. They would be sorry they'd cast me aside. I'm too beautiful for words, too beautiful for words. They'd realize their mistake and come begging. It was just a matter of time.

***

What can I say? The rest of July my owners were all aflutter, packing, boxing, tossing things out. While they gave me the routine daily scratch, the massages and brushings were a thing of the past. I don't want you to think I received cruel and unusual treatment. My owners were generally really kind people. It's just that they weren't terribly forward thinking. When they first adopted me, didn't they realize that pet adoption is like baby adoption, like THIS IS A FULL-TIME COMMITMENT!!! No thought to the future. No exit strategy! And they had me declawed, no less. Didn't they know that maybe a physically-challenged cat isn't as desirable? People can be so judgmental, so superficial. No one would want a handicapped cat!! I'd be alone, cast aside.

Wait, I need to catch my breath. The memory of that month still flusters me. Inhale, hold a moment, and release. Again, inhale, hold, release. Better.

One Saturday in August they took me to that place called the Humane Society. She was a little teary, he blasé but trying to comfort her. I lifted my head, angled it slightly to the right (my best profile) and with my tail in the air, I turned from them. *Fini, finito.* Never again. Very Sarah Bernhardt, if I say so myself.

The first night or so was hard. All alone. Even surrounded by my fellow prisoners, I felt hopelessly alone. And let me tell you, the Humane Society will *not* be the path to my formal societal debut. But you already know that, don't you? There's no need to mince words here. I'd been sent to the Big House. No room with a view. Dry food in a bowl, filled once a day. And so confining. The bidet right next to the food bowl. *Mon Dieu!* I'd been incarcerated, locked in a cell behind bars, sentenced without a trial. And while this was no Alcatraz (Wasn't Burt compelling in that role? His Birdman kept my eyes riveted to the screen!), it seemed I was there for the long haul.

At first I was really scared. I'd seen some of those "women in prison" made-for-TV movies. Scaaarrry! The good news, I suppose, is that I had my own cell so no fellow prisoner horror stories. No Toms or Thomasinas having their way with me.

And the guards? I maintained a cool, distanced demeanor to be on the safe side (those horror stories again). But they seemed rather nice and unassuming. And full of compliments, I might add.

Force of Nature

Penny's quite a pretty girl.

Look at those eyes. Gorgeous! She'll win someone over soon.

And a little extra attention did come my way during the day, but nothing untoward.

Time for a pet. Oh, look at that tummy. Penny needs a tummy rub!

I decided I could live with it for a while. It seemed I had no choice.

$$* * *$$

The visitors came, and the visitors went, but still no one seemed to want me. Another Sunday afternoon arrived. It seemed like a lifetime, but it had only been a couple of weeks. My backside against the cold bars, I contemplated ways to entertain myself. From a distance I heard the dayshift guard say, *"She's back."* A few moments passed. "Squish, squish, squish" on the linoleum floor. Sounded like running shoes, light weight, small frame. Footsteps enter my cellblock. Eight by ten with nine cages from floor to ceiling on both sides.

I sensed my fellow prisoners' alertness. Something different was at hand. Silence. She was right outside my cell. "She." Should I be concerned? Was she the prison matron, the person in charge? Up until then I'd only met the guards. More silence. I heard the turning of paper. Oh my gosh, if "she" is the matron, maybe I'm being transferred. But why would I be transferred? Unless I'm going to be....? Were they going to....? Does California have the death penalty? Would I be a dead cat walking? (Where's Susan Sarandon when you need her?) No, oh no. I hadn't been there that long. And I'd been good. And I was 100% healthy. My heart started to race. Stay calm. I had to stay calm.

Perhaps I should turn? I thought. No, I'll just wait and see. A few more moments and then I heard a soft, low voice. Sounded like she was reading something.

Name is Penny. White/gray domestic. Male. Neutered. Wait. Male? Tail long, ears erect, coat short. Short? Reason for surrender: Moved to a new place.

My ears were alert with attention. *Male? Neutered?* Not the last time I checked. *Short fur?* I don't think so. Who filled out those forms anyway? She couldn't be the boss. She must be one of the Big House visitors, but none have ever considered *me* before. Would she? Could she? Was it possible she was thinking of me to.....?

Indoor, declawed.

Would she care if I was declawed? And now had fleas? Or that my weight had dropped to seven pounds? Oh, what was wrong with me? I'm so nervous. Calm down, calm down.

More silence. It sounded as though she was kneeling, but I couldn't see. The voice was closer now, very calming, almost soothing.

Penny, the volunteers say you're very pretty, but I can't tell much from the back. You do have a lovely backside, but won't you turn around so I can see your face? Are you asleep? Come on, pretty girl, turn around.

Pretty girl? On such familiar terms so soon? Was this a trap? Luring me, reeling me in? Slowly—ever so slowly—I turned my head and gazed up.

A soft gasp and from out of the stranger's mouth I hear, *Oh my goodness, you're beautiful. Why, you're too beautiful for words, too beautiful for words!!*

I couldn't have said it better myself! Home at last, home at last. Thank God, I'd found a home at last!

Chapter Two

*　*　*　*　*

Chloe Anne

I felt such *kvelling* in my heart. Okay, I wasn't raised in a Jewish home, but I've always felt a certain kinship with the Chosen People. And *kvelling* says it all.

So, Penny, would you like to spend some time with me? Maybe get to know each other better?

I quickly rise, purring slightly and rubbing up against the cell bars. Absolutely!!

She calls for a guard and within minutes we're together in the jail's visitors' room. This is a special room in which the prisoners and potential guardians can size each other up. It has a large window and built-in bench seats. Toy mousies and balls are strewn on the floor.

This is a first for me as I've never been out of my cell since my arrival. What a treat! Initially I run around, then slow down to a stroll. I jump up on the window sill and nonchalantly stare into the distance. I don't want to appear too interested lest she think I'm desperate or too needy. Very unattractive! A bit of coyness with a sly over-the-shoulder glance. I also want to keep my excitement under control. I mean, what if she's only here to look? Maybe she's not ready to make a commitment. You know, a lot of relationships suffer from commitment issues. Dr. Phil did several episodes on this problem.

So, Penny, maybe you'd like to know why I'm here. A little bit about me?

Yes, for starters.

Well, I want to adopt a cat....

That I know. Move on.

And not just any cat. I've been looking for a while. In fact, I've been coming here on weekends for a few months.

So that's what the guards were referring to.

....so I'm looking for a special one. First, a female....

That's me.

...and one that is social, gets along well with others....

Me again.

But I'm pretty picky. You know, a girl has to have standards.

You have no idea.

Chloe Anne

Now, I have a kitty at home. Her name is Cinders.

Wait a minute. Another kitty? Competition!?! Cinders? What am I? Chopped liver? Chopped liver? Wait! I LOVE chopped liver!

Penny? You look pensive. Are you okay?

Perceptive. A good thing!

Come back, sweet face. Don't run away. Wait, let me sit on the floor. It's easier for me to see you. Much better. I know this is a lot of information at one time, but I want you to know everything.

Uh-oh, is "everything" what I really want to hear? Could this be a lot of emotional baggage?

Cinders used to belong to my mom, and I brought her home to live with me after my mother died. About 2 years ago...

Details, details. Why do humans think we're interested in the minutiae of their lives? Please. Just tell me where the food is, can I sleep on the bed and do you have HBO?

Has anyone ever told you how pretty your paws are? I know you're declawed. So is Cinders, but it doesn't matter to me.

Her voice is so calm, so soothing. But I wish I could check her references...have a chat with this Cinders. I may not be in a position to be too choosy, but I need to be sure.

...When I'm at work, Cinders listens to the radio...

Radio!

...I think the radio can get to be a bore, don't you? But she can't seem to get enough of it.

RADIO!

...so when I get home at night, we have playtime with the string and the laser light.

WHAT ABOUT TV!!?!

Now you don't look like a radio or laser light type of girl. Maybe I'm wrong about that, but I think you'd like the TV better.

Thank God! Is it a HD flat screen? A plasma? I've heard those are the best. And Cable? Do you have Cable? Please tell me you have the Platinum Package. I'd really like to see Animal Planet.

...Lots of channels to choose from. I'm sure you'll find your favorites. And we'll find some other activities for you. No need for either of you to get bored just because you have to stay indoors. There are always ways to have adventures, even if you can't go outside. Now, let's see. What else? Oh yes, food. I'd better check about your diet.

Diet? Do I look like I need to be on a diet?

You've only had dry here, but that's to be expected. Institutional food, if you know what I mean.

But of course! I wonder what other options she has in mind? Trout Amandine? Chicken Fricassee? Shrimp Scampi?

Your papers say your previous owners fed you canned food. But I think we'll do a combination of both dry and wet and go from there.

I was hoping for...hmmm, best to chat about this with Cinders before making any demands. There's power in numbers, you know.

So what do you think, Penny? Would you consider coming to live with us?

This must be a dream. Pinch me, please. I look at her, and I just can't believe it. I've felt so forsaken. Is this really happening? I need to let her know, but I don't want to appear too needy. Oh, this is hard. Just like Dr. Phil says it is...mustn't come across too strong but be true to your feelings. I also don't want her to doubt my feelings for a minute. Some purring. A little rubbing against her legs. Nudging her hand with my head. Scratch my cheeks, please.

My you're a slender girl. I can get my hands around your middle. Oh what a pretty girl. Now, I won't be able to take you home today.

Force of Nature

What? But, but...WHY NOT? WHY NOT TODAY?

No, no, no, don't run away. I need to get the house ready, that's all. But I'll fill out the forms and make sure a sign is posted on your cage door that you've been adopted. Nobody else can have you but me.

She calls for the prison guard, and I'm placed back in my cell. The walls start to close in. I start to hyperventilate, my heart racing again. Please, please, don't go. Take me with you. NOW!! How can I be sure you'll come back?

Ah, sweet face, don't look so sad. I'll be back in a couple of days. I promise.

A couple of days! No! Please no! I want to go with you now. I don't want to stay here. Please don't leave me here! Why don't you understand?

Chloe Anne

It's okay, Penny. Just a day or so. You don't have to worry.
I'll be back.

Oh, I feel dizzy. I bet no one's ever given you away before. I need...I need to know if you'll be back.

One last thing, sweetie pie. I hope you don't mind, but I
don't think the name Penny suits you. These soft and silky
tresses — your beautiful eyes — Hmmm. You know if I had
had a little girl of my own, I wanted to name her Chloe Anne
— Anne with an "e" — And it seems so perfect for you.
Would you like that? I hope you don't mind.

Mind? Mind? I tilt my head, beam and *kvell*. Time to start packing!

Chapter Three

* * * * *

Family...and Jewish Yet!

I t did take a few days, and yes, I did have a few more moments of anxiety. But return she did. I said my goodbyes, trying to give encouragement to the cellmates I was leaving behind. To the guards, a sweet meow. After all, I wasn't maltreated during my incarceration, and they were just doing their job. Everyone has to make a living.

I was carried out of the building not in the arms of my rescuer but in a cardboard carrying case. Not my preferred style of making an exit but apparently the jailhouse has regulations. No matter. There were holes through which I could see and sniff. And as we left the building, looking and sniffing were at the top of my list. The warm breezes of that August morning I'll never forget. The air on my nostrils...the sights passing by. And we were still walking across the parking lot! Not even to the car yet!

Now, Chloe, you have to stay in the box while I'm driving. I picked you up early today because we have one stop to make. We need to get you bathed because....

Bathed? Lost in the continued blissful reverie of freedom, my mind wandered.

A spa. What more could a girl ask for? An oasis of candles, lotions, aromatherapy. A warm tub in which to soak. Or better yet, just a little herbal steam with a dry brush massage. Something to relax and rejuvenate me. And get rid of these ridiculous fleas and my dry, flaky skin. A little exfoliation, please. What a treat this will be!

***

The car came to a stop, the door opened, and I was lifted out. I tried to see through the holes but to no avail. Through a set of doors and I guess into a reception area. Hmmm, the scent here is a bit odd. A little antiseptic. It must be one of those special treatments. Microdermabrasion or a glycolic scrub.

Chloe Anne is here for her bath. Yes, I'll wait to speak to him.

I hear a door swing open, and I can hear a male voice. Lower register. Confident, authoritative tone, calm. A man will be giving me my treatment? Well, as long as there is a paw treatment included, I'm game.

Valerie. It's good to see you again.

I'm all eyes and ears as the case is opened, and I find myself face-to-face with my aesthetician: Dark, curly hair. Deep, blue eyes. Thin wire rim eyeglasses. A beard, not so closely trimmed, a rather scholarly appearance for this type of job, but who am I to argue?

Well, Chloe Anne, let me look at you. Come out of this box. Let me see. Oh, but you are beautiful. Just gorgeous.

Up into his arms I'm lifted and hugged. Not a bad start for a treatment. Just go with it, Chlo, just go with it!

So, you have fleas? Yes, I see. Well, I'll take care of everything. I'll make you even more beautiful than you already are. Can you imagine that? Yes? No? Ah, Chloe Anne, we'll make it all better. Valerie, come back in three hours. She'll be ready then.

And with a swift turn, I'm carried off, through the swinging doors, hearing my owner's response in the distance, *Okay, you two, have a good time.*

A good time? Little did I know. Now, don't misunderstand. He was gentle, calming, everything I could have asked for in an aesthetician. In fact, I survived only because of his skilled hands and soothing words. Where shall I begin?

The lights. Glaring, fluorescent. Not the low-dimmed mellowness of any day treatment facility I had imagined.

Where is the meditative space of candles? And the new-age music? You know, Yanni or Enya. The stuff that Marin County or Berkeley thrives on. I mean, they may not be to my liking—I'll take Alejandro Fernandez any day—but this is Northern California for goodness sakes! My nose starts to twitch. The smell. Not like any potpourri I'm familiar with.

The institutional gray walls start closing in. Focus, Chlo, focus. He would never hurt you. Listen to HIM. Focus. Focus.

So, Chloe, let me tell you what we'll be doing: First, a comb-out. You have to be free of matting or knots. You have none? Still, we'll comb. Next, we'll clip your back claws. Yes, your mom told me about the declawing. Only the back paws. Ready? Now, a dip in the water. Not the head. No, no. A little shampoo and then a massage.

Well, all of this would have been well and good (He certainly had a way with the massage. Upper back, please.) but...the shampoo. Oh, my God! Oh, my God!

It must have been medicated. He didn't ask about allergies or skin sensitivities....not that I knew I had any of course. But still! Foaming at the mouth. You heard me. This was no Sheer Volume Pantene, no Ultra Moisturizing Nexus. Get me out of here. Get that stuff off of me!

Oh, no, no, no, don't worry. Everything will be fine. A little medicated soap. We're killing the fleas. We have to clean you up for your new home.

I stop dead in my tracks. Well, that's rather hard to do in a tub of water—particularly when one's paws aren't touching the floor. But you get the picture.

I think of what I've just heard. Clean for your new home? Your mom? Something else is happening here. Yes, I'm sure of it, but what is it? Where did I hear about this? Was it the History Channel? The combing of the hair, the clipping of nails, the immersion. I look up at him. Why, he's not an aesthetician. He's a rabbi! Yes, I'm sure of it now. This isn't a spa at all but...a *mikvah*!

Okay, so no prayers were recited, but hey, I'm a cat! And she wants me to be a part of her home, to be a member of her family. What else could this be?

See, the shampoo is done. Let's rinse. Warm water. Yes. Now, conditioner. Better? I think so. Time to dry: First the towel and then the air blower. Just like a full service salon for our Chloe. A little brushing and see? Beautiful fur and no more fleas. Your mom will be so happy. Feeling better now?

Better? Not only am I free of fleas, my skin moisturized and my fur conditioned, but the greatest gift of all: I'm now a Member of the Tribe. And you know what that means—I've got a *Jewish* mother! I wonder, does she know how to make *gefilte* fish?

Chapter Four

* * * * *

Taking the Position

The turn of a key in a lock. I'm inside a building. I feel myself being lowered, still in the carrying case. I hear a door shut, and I think I'm alone. I hear movement, a little talking, but nothing more. The atmosphere is calm, no sense to be alarmed. My anxiety level at zero, I settle in and wait. And ponder.

***

The door handle turns. Though I haven't been asleep, I'm not sure how much time has passed.

Chloe, I'm going to keep you in your box for a little while. There's not a problem, but I need the two of you to meet slowly. You know, get a scent of each other? I know you're cramped, but try to be patient. Cinders, come here.

I wait. There's movement outside the box. Pink nostrils appear in one of the holes and then disappear. Some pawing on the side but, as yet...wait. Hissing. Not a lot and not angry. Sounds like: "I know you're in there. Mom's told me about you."

Now, I understand what hissing is all about. Defensive posturing, setting boundaries and all that. But for me...well, hissing just isn't a part of my nature. I just don't do that type of thing. It's just not me. I guess I'm not much of a Darwinist or maybe spending all my time indoors has colored my perspective. Something akin to what that Rodney guy said. It was way before my time but the news media still makes reference to it—why can't we all just get along?

But I've digressed. I want out of this carrying case so I'll just rise above it. Just a soft...no, I'll make it plaintive...meow.

Silence. The nose again. And the pawing. More hissing. More pawing.

No, Cinders. Only smell. Don't try to knock the box over.

Knock the box over? Is she some sort of heavyweight? I angle my head up so my eyes reach the air holes. Simultaneously, as I look out, a green eye looks in. Startled and aghast, I pull back! My heart's going crazy. This is just too Jurassic Park for me. And with my sudden movement, too quickly and with too much force it would seem, the carry case tips and lands on its side. Humans say that a cat always lands on its feet, but what do they know? We're talking a confined compartment here. And while I'm not large (see Chapter Six), what feline could possibly maneuver a four-paw landing in such cramped quarters? No judge would ever give me a perfect 10 in such circumstances.

Cinders!! What have you done? Oh no!!

First and foremost, let me say that I never planned to have Cinders banished from the room. Let me emphasize she didn't get into trouble or was punished or anything. But, if I say so myself, it all worked out quite nicely in my favor. Mom just said: *Enough for now,* and took her out. The next thing I knew Mom pulled me from the case and onto her lap. Nuzzling my ear, scratching my cheeks, she repeated over and over: *Are you okay? Chlobo? Are you okay?*

I positioned myself on her lap, following the time honored Four Step Method:

· Step One: Whether jumping up on your own or being lifted, circle once (a full 360° turn), then sit with your hindquarters on your owner's knees, facing her (or him as the case may be....no gender-bias allowed).
· Step Two: Knead gently. I recommend skipping this step should you have claws. Remember, the objective is for both parties to feel comfortable.
· Step Three: Looking up at your owner, wait for a cheek scratch, kiss on the forehead and the inevitable (but not required): *How's my* [your name]?

· **Step Four:** Get up, leisurely turn in a circle twice (Again, the full 360°. Don't skimp!) and sit squarely on and between your owner's two thighs, head facing forward, looking outward. This provides for maximum petting and stroking and with the occasional neck and ear kisses.

We call this "Taking the Position." There are variations, of course, but this is the standard method.

Chloe, there's going to be some adjustment time over the next few days. For all of us. The way we're going to work this is simple. This will be your room for the next 24 hours. I put a litter box in the corner for you, and we'll keep the door closed overnight. But right now I want to go talk with Cinders and make sure she's okay. There's a little food over there in the bowl. Some water too. We'll be back in a few minutes.

Room confinement for 24 hours? I can do this. So what's of interest to me? The sofa could use a few more pillows, but it will serve nicely for an overnighter. No cat scent on it. Maybe Cinders doesn't sit here? Spread myself around a bit, if you know what I mean. A little sit here, a little sit there. No, maybe I should move to the other side. Hmmm, better where I was. You see, while I'm not into territorial hissing, I am a strong proponent of squatting rights. A little pawing here and there on a couch or chair (and remember, no claws so no damage to the furniture). Some stretching and rolling around. Done.

What else to note? Ah, the litter box. It smells very fresh. No one's used it yet. As it should be. And the food? Hmmm, a little different from what I'm used to but quite adequate.

Anything else? No, just human stuff. Wait! What's that on the floor? Next to the couch?

The Sunday *New York Times*!! Oh, to be up close and personal to it! I've dreamed of this moment! No, I don't read. Have you forgotten I'm a cat? But I wonder if it's a daily subscription. I just can't wait to sit on all the news that's fit to print. Particularly the Food Section on Thursdays. My slice of heaven!

The door opens and in comes Mom, holding Cinders. I can't believe I was so shell-shocked earlier. She's quite petite and, you know what, very pretty...in a tabby sort of way.

Chloe, this is Cinders. No more boxes. Just the three of us. I'm going to watch some T.V. and the two of you can sort things out.

She's pretty and petite. She has short fur and it's multicolored—brown, black, grey, traces of amber. Her chest and tummy are grey. Her tail is very beautiful. Kind of like a raccoon's....black and grey rings, circling all the way to the tip. Her face is quite delicate. But you know what's most obvious? It's her gaze, steady, calm, thoughtful. She's very intelligent. Mom says she's only five, but she looks...hmm, wise. She knows something that I don't. What can it be? Now I feel nervous. What can it be?

***

Mom's been watching T.V. now for about an hour. Cinders and I are still on opposite sides of the room. No fireworks. Maybe it's time to move in a little closer. I slowly stand, stretch a bit. I move to the couch. Cinders' eyes are alert, following my every movement. I jump up and sit to the left of Mom.

But then I stop, not moving any further or closer. Awkward, I sit. No longer sure of my place or what to do, I'm unable to move. I don't understand.

I wait and eventually, Cinders stands up, does a leisurely stretch, sits again and stares at me. Finally, she stands, ambles over to the couch, and without a moment's hesitation, jumps up on its arm, to the right of Mom. Turning once, a full 360°, she looks at Mom. She kneads the furniture a bit. Then, another two full circles, and she settles onto the couch arm. Mom raises her hand and strokes her head and the ridge of her nose.

Ah, how's my sweet potato pie? How's my love?

Cinders nudges at Mom's hand and gets a full-face caress. Her eyes turn to me, knowingly and with what seems to me permission. So I move slowly to Mom's lap. I circle once, a full 360°, and look at Cinders. Her head tilts, an almost imperceptible nod. I knead a bit. Again, my eyes seek Cinders'. Then, another two circles, and I nestle onto Mom's lap. I look to Cinders and understand now whose couch it is: both of ours...albeit with my older sister taking the rightful "upper" position. As well she should, of course.

Chapter Five

* * * * *

To Sleep, Perchance to Dream...
But First I'll Eat a Little Something

And so we settled into our routine. Cinders and I are on our own for the greater part of the days. We sleep, nosh a bit, and help each other groom. Now all these are very important feline traits but in our household they take on a greater significance. It's what Mom refers to as "A person has to have priorities in life" (This is often used in juxtaposition with "A girl has to have standards" but for the time being, let's stick to those priorities.).

***

SLEEP: Remember that while cats are supposedly nocturnal animals, in fact most cats sleep approximately 18 hours a day. Cinders and I are no exception, but generally we keep to ourselves and respect each other's private time and "space." (Remember, this *is* Northern California.)

So, what is sleep in the feline world? We don't take this subject lightly, you know. There's sleeping and then there's sleeping. Numerous subsets exist. You see, we enjoy sleeping but that's not to be confused with dozing, napping or slumbering. Inexplicably humans use the word "catnaps" which, unbeknownst to them, is not to be confused with our napping.

Generally speaking, dozing, slumbering and napping occur during the daylight hours. *Our* dozing is a light sleep and requires no prep. It can happen, if you'll pardon the pun, in a blink of an eye. It's never planned. I'm sure Cinders wouldn't mind my using her as our subject.

Let's say that it's a warm, spring afternoon. Clear skies and from the bedroom one can see miles into the distance. The sliding door is open, and a warm gentle breeze is wafting through. Cinders is sitting on the top of the wing back chair, just gazing outward. She had no real plans for the next hour or so, just sitting a bit and taking in the panorama. Her paws are underneath her, tail wrapped around her side and from a distance (well, even up close) she resembles a meatloaf or a rolled pot roast. The next thing she knows her eyes are half-closed. *Voila!* She's dozing! She's in a very light sleep, that floating place that we all love. Not here but not there either. Some humans use dozing synonymously with "nodding off." Maybe in their world, but not in ours. Or maybe even taking "forty-winks"? Uh uh. It's a doze, pure and simple. It's not meant to refresh us. In fact, most often we're awakened, startled if you will, out of the dozing-state by a noise...even the softest of nature. But we expect this. After all, we're dozing.

Slumbering is of a different nature...a bit more complex, a state that requires a bit of planning, but still not to be confused with sleeping (close but no cigar!). What planning, you might wonder? Well, a slumber state of unconsciousness is deeper than one of dozing so we can't be positioned on the back or arm of a chair or in someone's path. You see, with dozing our senses and reflexes are at the surface. We come to in that curious "blink of an eye." When we slumber...well, our reaction time is a bit slower. So it's important that we position ourselves in a relatively safe area. The seat of a chair works, in front of the fireplace on a cold winter day. And we don't approach the designated slumber area lightly. Sniff the designated spot and paw a couple of times. Circle once (counter-clockwise) and settle down. Although we can lie down, all curled up, slumbering more readily implies a more reclined posture. Stretched on one's side or, my personal favorite, lying on my back with tummy exposed. The front legs are thrown and stretched above the head; the rear legs stretched out as far as they can go. Somewhat risqué and daring...a bit like Marilyn Monroe on deep red velvet. But....well, I think in the privacy of one's home, one can do as one wishes. Wouldn't you agree?

Napping. It runs a close second to slumbering but the major difference is that slumbering is more luxuriant while napping is more efficient in nature. It still requires prep (the sniff, the paw, the circle), but napping has a goal. We need undisturbed rest at this time. Because while it's a daytime activity, the aim is to conserve energy. No disturbances, dead to the world. This means that either we're on the bed (usually dead center...no need to unnecessarily fall off), the couch or the floor. The purpose of napping? Why, to get ready for Mom's return, dinner, TV, treats, chin scratches, treats... maybe even some dessert? The only thing that can stir us is an earthquake (God forbid!) or the sound of Mom's key in the door. Wait, what's that I hear?

***

EATING: I can't help it. Thinking about Mom coming home and all that transpires with her arrival has pushed me to the eating aspect of our life priorities. Of course, one must eat. Otherwise we'd all be....well, dead. But as with sleeping, there is eating and there is eating. And as I am rather a connoisseur on this subject...you'll come to understand why soon enough... why not jump full-bore into it now.

We have the snack, the bite, the munch, the graze, the nibble, breakfast and dinner (no lunch in this household!), and most important THE NOSH. A whole hierarchy in the feline gastronomical universe.

Breakfast. I'll cut to the chase and tell you that it is THE most boring meal of the day. I know it's supposed to be the most important meal of the day, but...BOORRRING! Before Mom leaves for work, we get some wet food and a dish of dry cereal. That's it. We have no choice but to eat it all because, after all, we've been asleep all night (Please don't confuse this with our daytime sleeping habits that really aren't sleep at all. Remember?). We're hungry. But there isn't a lot of time, and quite frankly, I think it's because Mom doesn't "do" breakfast during the week. She'd rather sleep than get up. So it's always a rush out the door, and she's gone (after, of course, her hugs and kisses to both of us. It doesn't matter how much of a hurry she's in, she never short changes us.). She leaves us a bowl of dry for snacking during the day, but that's it during the week.

Snacking, you say? Isn't that the same as noshing? Although oftentimes used interchangeably, the subtle difference between the two is that one *noshes* on something truly delicious, something that one really craves. Snacking, on the other hand, is done to get through the day. I mean, think about the words: Doesn't noshing convey two arms that envelope you, something that makes your heart sing, fills you with *nakhes*? But snacking? You pick up a Frito. It's there so you eat it... and another and another. One so Eastern European, the other so all American. Not that I'm knocking the latter, but to nosh is bliss, to nosh is divine, to nosh is love.

And so we snack. In between dozing and the like. And before we know it, it's around 7:00 p.m., and a key is heard turning in the front door lock.

Cinders, Chloe, I'm home! Where are my girls?

Cinders takes her time coming down the hall. I, on the other hand, am right there. Perhaps it's because I still have thoughts about my unfortunate incarceration...will I ever get over the fear of abandonment?....or perhaps I just know what's coming next. And I'm there. Waiting, attentive and ready. For what, you may ask? Why, what else?

What would my girls like for dinner?

Shoes off, quickly changed into anything other than a dress, she's in the kitchen, rustling about. Drawers open and close as does the refrigerator door. Puttering and muttering.

What do we have here? What do we have?

Lest you think the two of us get excited over nothing, the options for dinner can be overwhelming. On a slow night (that is, Mom hasn't been to the store in a few days. These are usually Thursdays and Fridays) we get a big helping of IAMS wet....preferably chicken. But on Monday and Tuesday, right after a shopping weekend, we get not only the wet food but....are you ready for this....

baby food. You know, Gerber's 2nd stage. Sometimes chicken, sometimes beef. But the veal. Oh, my God, to die for!!!! ABSOLUTELY my favorite.

But, noshing, you ask, I thought it's important to you? Where does noshing fit into all of this? Well, not to disappoint. Our noshes come in two distinct forms. On a weekday evening, it's some of the freshly cooked chicken or salmon that Mom prepares for herself. A *bissel* here, a *bissel* there. Heavenly. And on weekends, the nosh of all noshes: Costco rotisserie chicken! Yes, that's right. She picks it up on Saturday morning, and we get to nibble off and on throughout the weekend. Cinders prefers the dark meat, but I'm not choosy. I'm just passionate about our Costco chicken. In fact, I think I can say that a nosh in our household is the best treat of all. Because they're those special foods that we're given for no reason in the world other than Mom loves us. Such *nakhes* flows through me!

∗∗∗

GROOMING: Cats generally have great natural grooming habits because we recognize that looking our best is to our advantage. It's not just because Cinders and I are females. All cats are like this (Now, of course, there are exceptions to the rule. Sometimes when a cat is sick or older, grooming goes out the window. But isn't that the same with humans?). We spend quite a lot of time taking care of ourselves, licking and combing. And, as always, there are different types of bathing experiences.

First, the face-cleanse: Although this can occur at any time, the face cleanse is primarily a post-eating activity. And this includes all eating, not merely full meals of breakfast or dinner. Snacks, noshes, treats...come one, come all.

We first move away from the food bowl, creating a healthy distance to begin our toilette. Preferably about five feet minimum, with our back to the plate (or to Mom if she in fact gave us a treat by hand.). We might even move into the next room. Although privacy isn't a big issue with the face cleanse, the separation of bowl and paw is.

We start with the mouth, repeated lickings to ensure we catch every last morsel. I mean, with Gerber's veal, who could blame us? Such a sublime treat we don't want to miss anything. Then, ever so gently, we take a paw, first the right, then the left, and depending on the eye, clockwise or counter, first at the temple and then slowly over the eye brow with a quick movement down over the eye itself. Again. And again. Next, the paw starts over the ear, down over the temple and swiftly over the eye. And finally, we aim for our chest, quick movements of our head and tongue, reaching down to make sure we haven't dripped or dropped a bit. To others this may seem like overkill, but our grooming is not known worldwide for nothing. Thoroughness is the key so this process can take the better part of 20 minutes.

Second, the pre-nap preparatory: We like to feel comfortable before taking a rest, of any form. Don't humans apply moisturizer before drifting off? Well, we don't go that far, but again, we always like to look our best. Now, the face cleanse is a solo activity (generally speaking...more about that in a minute). However, a pre-nap prep covers the whole body. So, Cinders and I usually help each other out. As dexterous as cats are, washing our backs poses a problem. So we don't hesitate to assist each other with the head, neck and back areas. Starting with the head and then working our way down. As to tummies and other areas (you know of what I speak—please keep in mind that *this* memoir is G-rated), we go solo.

I must confess that once in a while, no matter how diligent I am, I miss some of the wet food on my face. Also, because I have long fur and I'm curvy (yes, Chapter Six again), it is sometimes difficult to clean in those hard to reach places. Let it suffice that Mom is always quick with a soft, warm damped cloth to clean me up. Cinders doesn't seem to have these problems. Maybe it's because she's been independent for so long she tends to take care of things herself, rather than asking for help. But then again, she doesn't have the trouble that I do. How can that be?

Chapter Six

* * * * *

F* Is a Dirty Word

Well, I'll tell you. I'm a full-bodied girl. Some would say voluptuous, full-figured, *zaftig*. In fact, in a previous century, the word Rubenesque would be quite applicable. Today, BBW—big, beautiful woman—is a nice catch phrase.

How did I get this way, you may wonder? I was really quite slender when Mom adopted me. Her two hands could span my mid-section. How did this happen? Two words say it all:

FOOD NETWORK!!

Now, I think I've mentioned that Cinders loves the radio. I, on the other hand, am a product of television. Prior to my unfortunate incarceration, I was allowed to watch TV but the pickings were slim (My, how I love a good pun!) because the only cable station they would watch was CNN. So I settled for network programming and became a big fan of *The West Wing, Grey's Anatomy, Boston Legal.* But now the joys of cable TV! Too numerous to count: Animal Planet, H&G, TNT (I'm not sure that they know drama but I watch anyway), *TLC,* Jon Stewart and Stephen Colbert, continuous reruns of *Law & Order* (Jerry Orbach...now, I'd love to have him pat me down!), *Sex & the City, What Not to Wear.* The list can go on and on, but it all comes down to:

FOOD NETWORK!!

The Barefoot Contessa (How bad can that be? Not bad at all, Ina, not bad at all. And by the way, I LOVED your Friday night menu of brisket with carrots and onions. And not to forget the chopped liver and salmon with lentils. Yum!), *Everyday Italian* (Giada, your recipes and cooking talents speak for themselves.), *Molto Mario* (Now, I bet no one teases you about your size!), and of course my absolute favorite—*Boy Meets Grill* or *Throwdown* (Bobby Flay, you're cute, sexy, a little bit of attitude, charming, a mischievous smile and oh, did I forget to mention? WHAT A COOK!!! I'd have you prepare my meals ANYTIME. But if you don't want to cook for me, could you at least come rub my tummy or give me a chin scratch?).

Okay, the point is that Mom would watch Food Network in the evenings or tape the Saturday and Sunday shows. And I would watch alongside her. Literally, side-by-side, taking it all in. The difference is that Mom kept her weight under control. Still a size 6. And Cinders remained a slender 7 pounds. I, on the other hand, started to gain. Slowly, from 8 pounds up to 9 and then 10. Not a fast gain. Barely noticeable until I'm suddenly...18 pounds!! And it wasn't as though Mom was feeding me extra. Uh uh. Osmosis, transference—call it what you will—but the common thread leads back to:

FOOD NETWORK!!

I think my curves are to be admired, even desired. But truth be told—and it must be told—people tend to judge others based on their physical appearance and not on who they are inside. A generalization, I know, but there is a lot of truth in it. So even though Mom always tells me I'm her "big, beautiful girl," I know that others may find fault with my curves.

Why even Aron and Noah have been brainwashed. Even they have their biases and sometimes, I shudder to admit this, they can be unkind. Noah and Aron, you ask? Who are Noah and Aron?

They're my cousins. Well, not in feline terms, but Mom calls them that. They're Uncle Mike's and Aunt Sunny's (again, Mom's words) sons. Mom loves them so-o-o-o-o much.

EXCEPT WHEN THEY USE THE F* WORD!!

You see, in our house, we have rules. Really they're Mom's rules, and while a few of them might be a bit quirky (no TV in the bedroom, no dirty dishes left in the sink at night, keep the screen doors latched at all times), Cinders and I are okay with them. Anyway, one of her rules is that the F* word is not to be used in the house. Not under any circumstances. She knows that she can't control what happens once a person ventures outside, how one acts, what one says, but for whatever time we're in the house, we should each feel safe and secure. You see, it's her retreat, her nest, her home. It's a place in which no one's feelings should be hurt, in any shape or form.

So you can imagine how shocked the three of us were when the boys...well, let me tell you about it. The month was April, and Mom decided it was time for my "coming out."..my society debut, if you will. Not everyone had met me and with spring in the air, the timing seemed right. I think the party coinciding with the Passover Seder was just that, a coincidence, but with Pesach being the Festival of Freedom and my recent release from the Big House...well, it was all serendipitous if you ask me.

I had quickly learned during the first few months with my new family the emphasis the Jewish faith places on food. But admittedly I didn't fully grasp its significance until now. It doesn't matter if you're Orthodox, Conservative, Reform, Humanist, whatever: The bottom line is that if you don't love food, you couldn't possibly be Jewish. It's not one of the Ten Commandments (I still don't understand why Charleton Heston didn't work it into his negotiations with the Bush...the flaming one, that is.), but I'm sure it's somewhere in the Talmud.

Celebrating Pesach is a family favorite and to have a party for me at the same time was icing on the cake. For Mom it's because of wonderful childhood memories—large Seder gatherings with grandparents, aunts, uncles and cousins, family recipes and stories, laughter—in Tevye's word, tradition! And for Cinders and me, the glorious aromas coming from the chicken—oops, I mean kitchen—the accidental droppings of brisket on the floor, the....oh, I'm just so excited, I'm getting ahead of myself.

My party, as with any large society event, required much preparation: planning the menu, cleaning the house. I could go on and on. The invitations went out a couple of weeks before the soiree, and all the guests had RSVP'd they would be attending. The day before the party, as Cinders and I were sitting on Mom's bed immersed in our grooming, we heard the key in the front door. Nothing unusual there, but then we heard a big, booming, deep, male voice.

Where's the girl? Where's the girl?

Well, in a word, Cinders freaked and was under the bed in a flash (She's not really a people person.). Me? A male voice? *You* do the math.

I jumped off the bed and peered down the hallway. In the living room a man stood, his girth matching his voice. His back was to me, and he was looking around. I took a few steps and placed myself squarely in the middle of the hall. His head turned, and our eyes met.

So you must be Chloe. What a beauty! V, she's a big girl. Come here, come here. Uncle Jon wants to say hi.

The "big" part didn't register, but the "beauty" did. This man has taste. This Uncle Jon. I sauntered into the living room, keeping close to the walls. Mustn't appear too friendly. A girl has to have standards. Though I had stopped looking at him directly, I could feel his eyes on me. I sashayed slightly and coyly tossed him a glance over my right shoulder. I jumped up on a chair, the one directly in front of the window.

Immediately to my right was the fireplace and a Rothko print, the purple-black tones providing a nice contrast to my grey white fur.

Okay, no rush. I'll wait. Maybe a little playtime later. After dinner. V, where's Cinders? Under the bed? Cinders, come on out. You remember me? Uncle Jon.

He turned and went down the hallway to the bedroom.

Though a bit taken aback, I gave him credit. No lunging, grabbing, trying to pet without even a proper introduction. It's clear he'd been around animals before.

Val, she won't come out from under the bed. Still skittish?

Give her some time. She doesn't remember you.

With that, he returned to the living room, sat down on the sofa and waited. It became a test of wills. Who would make the first move? His gaze was intent, and he kept making cooing sounds to attract my attention. For a while he would converse with Mom, catching up on everything, but then he would return his focus on me. Minutes passed, the tension mounted.

Inside my stomach was in knots. He really knew his way around cats. It's not that I come hither and yon for every man (well.....), but finally I couldn't take it any more. Slowly I rose, nonchalantly stretched, did a quick face-cleanse and then gracefully moved to the couch. I rubbed a bit against his legs and jumped up next to him.

So what's going on, Chloe? Tell me what's new. Want a chin scratch?

And with that...Well, I don't kiss and tell.

✳✳✳

The rest of the day was uneventful. Mom made dinner and while the two of them ate, Cinders came out from the bedroom. It was clear that Uncle Jon held a special fondness for her and she for him. They go a way's back, with Grandma Peggy and all. She wouldn't let him get too close, but she glowed hearing his compliments.

***

It's time. My party. The Seder. We weren't allowed to help Mom at all. She banned Cinders and me from the kitchen but that's okay because we had much to do ourselves. Our grooming took the better part of the day. Head to tail. We wanted to look our very best.

Even though the event didn't officially start until sunset, the guests started arriving around 3:30. I was in my glory, basking in the attention of friends and family: Uncle Rodney—great fun. Always knows how to show a girl a good time. He's our #1 sitter when Mom is out of town. Loads of tummy rubs—done with his feet yet!—and always an extra treat before bedtime (Shhhh, don't tell Mom!). Anyway, sitting close to him during the meal was a priority for me.

Aunt Jean: Mom's next door neighbor and one of her closest friends. I love her grasp of pop culture and the Hollywood bon mots that she sprinkles into her conversations are riotous. But I must confess, she can be strict and there was an episode...well, let it suffice for now that Aunt Jean is my #2 sitter. More about that later.

At around 4:30 the front screen door opened and in came Uncle Mike, Aunt Sunny and these two, tall young men. I guessed in their mid-teens. I quickly figured out that the two boys were their sons, the infamous Noah and Aron.

Noah: A slender redhead with what appears to be a sensitive demeanor. Soft-spoken. He immediately greeted Mom with an embrace and a kiss. Mom says he just got accepted to Cornell so he must be smart.

Aron: Younger, maybe fourteen, and thinner than Noah but the same height. He's blond and seems, at first glance, mischievous. I don't know why I think so, but I just think he likes to joke and tease. Does he have a sensitive side?

Well, time will tell because I was so thrown by what happened next, any further introductions will have to wait. Let me try and relate what transpired, but please understand that this was so jarring to my system I may have to pause to catch my breath.

As I said, the door opened and pleasantries between the adults were exchanged. At that time I was comfortably sitting in the hallway where I could get a good view of the arrivals. Not to mention, I was out of harm's way and foot traffic. Cinders had chosen to stay in the bedroom, hidden beneath the bed. I was looking up, perhaps expectantly, for a warm introduction. How shocked I was to hear from Aron:

Is this Chloe? Gosh, she's Fat!! Aunt Valerie, she's Fat!

Without even a hesitation, Mom was all over him. *Excuse me, excuse me?? Aron, we don't use that word in this house. Where are your manners?*

But, Aunt V., she's Fat. Look how big she is!

And then from Noah, *You know, Aunt Valerie, he's right.*
She IS pretty large.

Enough. Both of you. She's voluptuous. A full-bodied girl.
But don't use that word in this house. Just stop it.

Hey, I only speak the truth. And she's one Fat cat. So where's
Cinders? And stepping over me, Aron headed towards
the bedroom.

I don't know what to say. I felt so wounded. I had
been so excited about meeting both of them, and I just, I
just.......This was supposed to be such a special evening.
How would I make it through the festivities? Leslie Gore
was so right. It was *my* party, and I wanted to cry.

I moved to the wall, crouching as close as I could,
trying to disappear. But how can an F* cat disappear? I
was only 11 pounds at the time. What were they seeing
that I couldn't? My breathing quickened, and I started
to hyperventilate. "I'm too beautiful for words. I'm too
beautiful for words." It wasn't working. Nothing was
working. A full-blown anxiety attack was coming on

strong. As the darkness started to envelope me, I heard a faraway voice.

You know what, Chloe? I think we need to check out what Mom is serving tonight? And without further ado, Uncle Rodney swept me up, and we went to the kitchen. The aromas got stronger with every step, and I was thankful that Uncle Rodney knew the right smelling salts to revive me.

Look, Chlo, we're having brisket and gefilte fish. You know, I'm not too fond of the fish. Would you like to share mine? Maybe we could sit together?

I peered out over his arm and saw a panoply of gastronomical delights: brisket resting on the countertop, dripping in gravy made with onions, chile sauce and garlic. A stock pot filled with chicken soup and matzoh balls, plates laden with fish topped off with dollops of horseradish. My eyes widened, my nostrils flared. No drooling but close to it. The unnecessary aspersions were a thing of the past.

And so we gathered together at the table, I on the floor, nicely ensconced between Uncle Rodney and Uncle Jon. Cinders had come out to join the festivities but chose to sit just a few paces out of reach. I heard Aron and Noah comment about her size also. (*Cinders, you're Fat...I mean, you're bigger than last time. You're shaped like, like a....pear.*) I glanced at her and her eyes said it all: "They're boys. Ignore them." I just don't know where she gets her strength. How does she not let it bother her?

Mom lighted the festival candles, her voice quivering with emotion. So many memories for her. Uncle Mike led the Kiddush and then the story of Pesach began. I sat patiently, listening to the telling: the Four Questions, the history of the Exodus, the sharing of the ritual food. Patiently, so patiently until I heard Uncle Jon proclaim, *Let's eat.*

Let the fun begin!! Cinders quietly made her way to the other side of Uncle Jon's chair. And then, for the next hour.....

Rodney, please don't feed them! They'll have their own food in the kitchen later.

I'm not (Chlo, try a little fish. Store bought stuff. Not homemade, but you might like it.)

Jon, what's going on down there? What are you doing?

Nothing (Cinders, have some chicken. There, on the napkin. You don't like white meat? Here, a little dark.).

Chloe, Cinders, don't beg. You'll have dinner later.

They're not begging. They're being perfect kitties (Chloe, a little brisket? No, don't eat the onion. You like the onion? Okay. A little more meat. What a good girl.).

Stop it, you two. They'll be impossible from now on.

We're not doing anything (Your mom's getting testy. Let's chill for a minute. Oops, was that a piece of brisket jumping off my plate? Go for it, Chlo, go for it.)!

What can I say? A slice of heaven for both of us. After the meal, during the service conclusion, I had hoped to search for the *afikomen*. But the two of us were so full, so content, we took our leave. Into the bedroom and up among the pillows, we curled against each other and fell into a blissful, sated stupor.

***

A voice. Then two. Sleep filled the room. Oh, please, don't disturb me. I don't want to move. I don't want to wake up. The voices grew clearer. *Chloe, it's Aron. I'm going home now. Want to say goodbye.*

Chloe, it's Noah. Wake up a little. We want to talk to you. And Cinders too.

I was curled against a pillow, with Cinders' backside to my left. I opened one eye and noticed that the night lamp had been turned on. I stretched my right-front leg and closed my eye. Burrowing my nose into the pillow, I again heard, *Chloe, Cinders, wake up a little. We don't have a lot of time.*

Opening my eye again, I saw two sets of blue eyes, up close and personal. Oh, no, *now* what?

You know, I think you need to know something. First, we're really happy that we finally got to meet you. Aunt Valerie talks about you all the time, how you and Cinders really hit it off, how you make her laugh, how much she loves you....

Where is this going?

Yeah. But when we visit Aunt Valerie, we always like to see if we can get her to react to things. It's kind of funny. Très amusant.

Tu parles français?

Chloe, what Aron's trying to say is we used the F* word to give Aunt Valerie a bad time. We know she doesn't like it, but where would we be without a little light-hearted teasing?

Force of Nature

Things just got out of hand, and you didn't know what was going on.

Yeah. Maybe we went too far. But we want you both to know that we definitely don't think of either of you that way. You're both pretty special.

Okay, so it's not Yom Kippur. But isn't it best to forgive and forget? And I do have a soft spot for men who know how to apologize. Purring like Mom's car running in neutral, I stretch out, all legs reaching their furthest. I turn my green eyes to meet their blues and nuzzle their hands in appreciation. Hmmm...Do I smell *charoset?*

Chapter Seven

* * * * *

Look What the Cat Brought In

I don't recall when going outside started to appeal to me. It must have been during the spring or summer months when the back door was open, and I could look out through the screen door. I could see birds flying from any window in the house. There was something about the fresh air hitting my face and the smells and noises that peaked my interest.

I'm fairly sure that Mom picked up on it, particularly because I started asking to go out.

Stop pawing at the screen, Chlo.

More pawing.

You can't go outside, Chlo. Don't even think about it.

A little more pawing.

Stop it, Chloe.

Pawing with a full-body press against the door.

Chloe Anne, get away from the door. How many times do I have to tell you? You CAN'T go outside!!

But persistence is one of my finer traits. Not to mention curiosity. Hello!?! I'm a cat!! And while I was first taken by the smells and noises, I must admit noticing something that mesmerized me. It was just too tantalizing to ignore.

The Duck

You see, there's a lagoon outside our house. And it's big. I could see this group of ducks swimming around all the time, but I kept noticing one in particular. I don't know why, but it stood out from the rest. What's its story? If only I could get a closer look.

I know the pawing was driving Mom crazy, but I've found that sometimes she gives in when pushed just a little bit. I could only hope. I mean, *a duck!*

✳✳✳

I mused, I pondered, and I continued to paw at the door.

If you're so insistent, Chlo-bo, I'll take you out myself. We'll just take a walk around the deck for a few minutes.

It's a start. Patience, patience.

She picked me up and out we went. The day was clear, and the sunlight intense. She carried me around the deck, showing me the flowers. Very nice, very nice, but let's go near the water.

Obviously her thoughts were elsewhere because the next thing I knew she sat down, placing me squarely on her lap. I took The Position with great anticipation, knowing that when I settled in, I'd be looking straight out at the water. Comfortably situated, I lifted my eyes and saw...a hedge!

Better, Chloe?

No.

This was a good idea.

Not as good as it could be.

Just a few more minutes. Are you enjoying yourself?

Well, to be honest, I was. And realizing that I wouldn't meet my objective this time around, I decided to relax. Not to mention that being on my best behavior might give Mom a reason to bring me outside again. And as if she was reading my mind, I heard: *You've been such a good girl. Maybe we'll do this again soon.*

Ah, progress!

***

We went out a few more times, and as luck would have it, Mom took me to the water's edge. She held me so my movements were limited, but all the better because The Duck was oblivious to my presence. I could observe it and its friends unnoticed.

Intriguing. They were always on the water, swimming the length of the lagoon and back. Making quite a racket with their quacking. A noisy group. I had seen them take off and land, always on the water, but to and where from I had no idea. And they ate out there, too. I saw them feeding on the surface. Or sometimes reaching as deep as they could underneath, up-ending without completely submerging. What balance and breath control! Incredible!

But I never saw them on land. I wondered: Do ducks walk? If it looks, quacks and swims like a duck, it must be a duck. No mention of walking so I guess they don't. On the water, 24/7...what a life!

✳✳✳

Could I help it that Mom left the screen door ajar that morning? An optical illusion? No, it was clearly unlatched. So unlike her, but who am I to pass up this monumental opportunity? I looked all around me. I was alone. I moved to the door. Perhaps if I leaned ever so gently? Yes, it is open. Again, I look to the right. To the left. Then over my shoulder. The coast is clear. Nudging slowly but firmly, the door opens and I'm out!

I ran to the deck's edge and came to an abrupt halt. The feeling was overwhelming: As if I was locked in a room stocked with open canisters, filled with salmon, chicken and beef treats. I had no limits. Unencumbered freedom. My choices were endless.

I looked again behind me, checking the door. It had closed without a sound. I didn't hear Mom calling for me so my absence wasn't noticed yet. But she didn't need to worry. The DNA of Elsa, Simba and Tony the Tiger is in my blood. I can handle anything or anyone that comes my way.

I moved off the deck and onto the lawn, sniffing every blade of grass. Oops, someone's poop. How gross! It must be from a dog. No upstanding cat would leave any telltale signs. I made my way to the hedge on my left, and crawled stealthily under it. I preferred being on the lawn, but I knew that remaining there left me very exposed. I continued to crawl, the ground soft and cool beneath my paws. Coming to the other end of the hedge, I paused and looked out. All was quiet. A few birds here and there, but they didn't hold any interest for me. Today it was The Duck, pure and simple. Where was it?

***

I awoke to quacking. Had much time elapsed? I heard no calls from the house, and the sunlight was still bright. A short doze, but no matter. The time was ripe, and my game plan simple: This would be an initial fact-finding mission. I'd have others in the future, I'm sure.

I moved slowly out from under the hedge, but still close to it for coverage. I checked for friend or foe in the immediate vicinity. Safe. Then, I moved to the water's edge to observe the gaggle.

All went well, and again, luck was with me. The Duck was among them. As always, it was at the tail end of the group. Was it the runt of the family? Or perhaps it was the strongest and therefore the rearguard? Hmm, strength is always an attractive trait. Wait! The Duck was falling behind the crowd. Something's amiss. I stayed crouched close to the ground and motionless. It broke off from the rest and started swimming towards the shore. This is fabulous. This was more than I could ask for. Just me and The Duck, land and water, examiner and examinee. With a little private observation....

Chloe, where are you? Are you out here? Chloe?

Startled, I looked quickly over my shoulder. It was Mom. Should I respond? No, I had come so far. I knew she was worried, but just a few minutes. I needed a little more time.

My head darted back to The Duck, and I hoped my sudden movements were undetected. It was still swimming in my direction. Certainly it would stop soon or turn around? Where else could it go? What? It's not stopping! It's not stopping! What? It's coming out of the water! Oh my God, it's walking!! It can walk! The Duck can walk!! It's a miracle!

It stopped to shake the water off its feathers and then continued towards me. It had sensed my presence and noticed my movements. Was it really interested in me? Was it angry? Was it just curious? Why didn't it stop? Startled and flustered, my fur swelled. I crouched down, my ears back and my tail waving back and forth. That would keep it at a distance. The Duck's place was in the water, not on dry land. But before I could bring forth a growl, I heard Mom again, and her voice was filled with urgency and concern.

Chloe, this isn't funny. Chloe? Chloe!!

The Duck too stopped in its tracks. We looked in the voice's direction and then back at each other. Again, to the voice. A mother's concern. The Duck picked up on it and my hesitation and moved in until we were close enough to touch. I backed off, yet it kept coming, slowly and purposefully. Before I knew it, it had backed me up against our deck. We weren't just close enough to touch. We did. Or rather, it did. Bill to nose, The Duck nudged me. Oh my God, it's going to bite me! What was I waiting for? I bolted and ran up to the screen door, pawing frantically to get back in.

Chloe, where have you been? How did you get out?

As she held me close, I nestled my head in her neck.

I was so worried, so scared. What if something happened to you? What if...??

She stopped mid-sentence. I looked up and saw her looking, no longer at me, but over my shoulder to the outside.

What in the??...There's a duck on our deck! How did it...???

I looked over my shoulder and saw The Duck. It was standing at the deck's edge, just where I left it in my moment of panic. Calmly, just waiting. Mom walked outside, still holding me. My heart was racing. Still, The Duck didn't move. Our eyes met, and our glances locked. Though space was between us, it tilted its head forward, and its bill, again, nudged me towards home... and Mom. And without so much as a quack, it turned and waddled back to the water. Silence until...

Chloe Anne?

I looked up at Mom. *Duck? What duck?*

Chapter Eight

* * * * *

A Dancing Queen

What's my exercise of choice? Considering my shape, style, and natural comportment, I think it's a given. I dance.

Shocked? You shouldn't be. But don't be mistaken. I'm not talking "freestyle-I'm-on-one-side-of-the-room-and-my-partner-is-on-the-other" dancing. Certainly not. I'm a ballroom dancer. I do all of them, but the waltz, rumba and quick-step are my favorites. It provides tremendous aerobic exercise. And it all began because Mom needed a practice partner.

***

I sat contentedly on the couch in the living room, listening to the music and watching Mom move up and down the hallway, practicing her rumba to Simone's "Yolanda." The CD was set on "repeat" and you'd think that hearing the same track over and over again would wear on one's nerves. But between Simone's deep, rich contralto, the melody and the lyrics, I never get tired of the song. Oh, my heart swells just thinking about it. Some people prefer "Besame Mucho," but it doesn't hold a candle to....but, I digress.

Mom was using an "air" partner, sorting out the moves, perfecting the steps. She had been going at it for about 25 minutes. It was now just a matter of time so I patiently waited and hoped. Yes! About fifteen more minutes passed and then she stopped mid-step. She turned to me, offering her hand, asking, *Would you like to dance, Chlo-bo? I need a partner.*

Would I like to dance? I rose quickly, she swept me up and off we moved around the room, weaving in and out around the living room furniture. I was flying above the clouds and feeling a natural high. My imagination took hold....

***

We've just been introduced to the audience, and we are the third couple to dance. No matter. We know that we are the crowd's favorite. I'm a little nervous…It's always a bit scary getting up not only in front of a live audience but knowing that our performance is being broadcast live to millions across the country. After all, *Dancing with the Stars* is a mega-hit.

We move to the center of the dance floor. I decided for the occasion that less is more and so I'm wearing just my grey-white fur coat with a simple diamond tiara on my head. Nothing more but an exquisite contrast to my green eyes. The outfit is a statement unto itself. And my dance partner has shown, yet again, what a truly class act he is, wearing basic black and letting the spotlight shine on me alone. He is, after all, my Che, my Zorro…my Antonio…I would expect no less.

You can't imagine how excited I was to learn that the program's producers wanted me on the show. And before I even thought to ask, they told me that they planned to pair me with Antonio Banderas. A perfect complement, they said. Would I mind? Ever calm, ever cool and always collected, I let them know it would be a pleasure (inside my heart was racing with excitement—a dream come true). And so we met and practiced, practiced, practiced. I had heard that Melanie is the jealous type, but those gossips are so wrong. She was so proud of both of us, particularly after we won the first two rounds.

The audience is momentarily subdued, in quiet anticipation of what awaits them. Left paw on his right shoulder and the right one in his hand, I cast my eyes over his shoulder as the dance requires. His right hand and arm have encircled my mid-section, bringing me close. I know he's looking at me. An inaudible yet pleasurable gasp escapes from my mouth, but I don't lose my stance or composure. There's too much at stake. The music begins, and we move as one.

Starting with a forward basic and an underarm turn, we move into quarter turns. Next into an open promenade, another quarter turn, the sweetheart (I'm in heaven as he holds me, but too quickly turns me out.). Alemanas, spot turns, and several hip rocks for good measure. A few more forward basics, underarm turn and then forward into closed position and his arms. Our eyes lock, and the music ends. There is a moment of stunned silence, and I can hear my heart pounding. Can he hear it too? No matter, because in a split second, the audience bursts into applause. The sound is deafening.

I'm overwhelmed by the response but make no show of it. The crowd loves us, but what about the judges? As we move stage left, we know this will be the moment of truth.

Again, you show us the true meaning of Cuban motion. Chloe Anne, you can't be new to the dance world. Your footwork is just too good for a novice. I give you a 9. I meow to Carrie Ann....appreciative of her remarks. Besides, she has two first names too. I would only expect positive comments from her.

Chloe Anne, you have style, panache. But your posture fell twice when your eyes looked down so I'll have to mark you down for that. But an above-average rumba performance. Score? 8. Len is always a bit of a stickler with the contestants.

But can you blame him? His standards are high. I'll just have to aim higher if we make it to the next round.

An 8? What? What? Never! Which dancers are you rating? Chloe and Antonio, ignore him. Your dancing is perfection on earth. You sizzle, you shine. I felt the passion and sensuality with your every move. Rumba is the dance of love, and the two of you have captured it. Brava! Bellisima! I give you a 10!! Bruno is standing up, waving his arms. A passionate Italian if ever there is one, and it seems the audience is behind him 100%. They won't stop cheering.

As we leave the stage, to make room for the next couple, I hear strands of "El Que No Lhora No Ama" playing. Antonio takes me again into his arms and we samba off the dance floor...

✳✳✳

...There wasn't much room in the living room so Mom's and my samba was danced with limitations. But we managed a few steps, and then it was time to rest. My heart rate was up, in a good aerobic way so it was time to cool down. I moved into the den and did the necessary stretching and bathing after a good workout. Then, settled into the corner of the couch, I drifted into a luxurious slumber...

Winning *Dancing with the Stars* opened doors for me. I was approached to do a yoga video, but there are just too many "dog" poses to my liking. Pass. And then a movie: A remake of *Sunset Boulevard*. Some hot shot producer thought I'd be perfect in the Gloria Swanson role. But something about the line "I AM big. It's the pictures that got small." just doesn't feel right coming from me. Perhaps I take things too literally for my own good, but I have to be true to myself. And as those of us in the business know, that can be so difficult to do.

No, I'm a dancer. So when I was called about rotating into "Cats" for the national tour, I jumped at it. Okay, it's not Broadway but what an opportunity! We packed quickly and left for New York. Only two weeks of rehearsal, and then I'd be on the road and under the lights.

Chloe Anne

Suffice it to say, rehearsal was hard work, demanding and intense, but work I did. And the moment arrived. The curtain is about to go up. My paw pads are little clammy, but I'm ready for the Jellicle Ball and more....

***

Chloe, don't take up the whole couch. Move over. "Ellen" will be on in five minutes.

I open an eye. What? And close it again.

***

....Our next guest first astounded the nation with her riveting dance performances on "Dancing with the Stars." And then she moved on to the National tour of "Cats"; capturing everyone's heart as I'm sure she will capture ours. Please welcome Chloe Anne.

I made my way onstage, head and tail held high. It was quite a thrill to be a guest on *The Ellen DeGeneres Show*. I had received offers from several of the late night hosts, but the terms of the appearances just weren't to my liking. One even requested I do a trick! Did the producers think I was stupid? No, Ellen's show was my first choice. She loves to dance and she's truly animal friendly. A win-win proposition, if ever there was one.

Well, Chloe Anne, let me first say that I'm speechless. You're even more beautiful in person than the TV cameras project.

(Thanks, Ellen. That's very flattering.)

Now, uh, I thought we could just take care of one subject. You know, get it over from the old get-go. There were rumors flying around about you after "Stars" first few episodes. Something about your misleading the show's producers: I think the tabloids reported that, contrary to the terms of your agreement, you did in fact have a number of years of dance training behind you. Of course, I don't read the tabloids.

(Of course not, Ellen. I know you don't involve yourself with tawdry gossip. But I appreciate your bringing this up as the rumors and gossip were just hurtful. No, I've never danced before. I was strictly an amateur. But, as I'm sure you know, with the right lead, any amateur dancer looks like a million dollars out on the floor. I was so fortunate to have Antonio as my partner.)

Well, I'm glad we cleared that up. Now, from there you moved to a national touring company. "Cats," was it? I saw the show—your performance—and I must say you were sensational.

(Thank you, Ellen. That means so much coming from you. I've always admired your dance style. The tour was just a dream of a lifetime. I was so blessed to be given the opportunity. And everyone was so wonderful to me.)

But, Chloe, there's that other subject floating about in the news. Now, you know I mean no disrespect, but what about the talk regarding you and Rum Tug Tugger?

(But Ellen, you know that I've been spayed.)

Stuttering and sputtering: *Well, is it true then that you've been offered your own show?*

(We're only in discussions at the moment, but I think I can safely say that one channel...quite animal friendly if you get my drift...has approached me. The proposal is a talk show, kind of a coffee klatch format hosted by five of us. Each of different ages and breeds to discuss various subjects....serious or light...but most important, topical.)

Anyone we know?

(Some names we've tossed about include Thomasina, Grizabella, Jennyanydots. But nothing's definite yet.)

Well, I hope you'll keep us in the loop and if it comes to fruition, we'll look forward to watching it. Any other news you'd like to share? It seems this sudden popularity must be a bit overwhelming.

(Yes, Ellen, I am a bit overwhelmed, but I always try to remember what my Mom tells me: You're in a fortunate position now, Chloe. Enjoy it, but success can be fleeting. Never forget from where you came.)

It sounds like you have a pretty smart Mom. Chloe Anne, you are a delight. It's been a pleasure having you with us today. Come back again soon.

***

…Chloe, what are you dreaming about? I don't remember you ever making noises while you sleep. What's going on in that head of yours? Come on, "Ellen" is over. Let's have dinner.

Chapter Nine

* * * * *

When Mom's Away....

It's Tuesday, and Mom's at the office. It seems autumn has arrived because the weather has gotten a bit nippy. Cinders is napping in the bedroom, Usually I'd snuggle in, but today I feel the urge to move about. What's happening in the closets? Hmmm, all the doors are shut. Under the bathroom sink? Can't get into the vanity. The computer is off so no fun to sit on the keyboard. What's to do at the other end of the house?

Pretty uneventful on this front too. What to do, what to do? My eyes move from the couch to the coffee table, past the fireplace, to the window and into the dining room. Wait! I turn my head sharply, and my eyes are back to the fireplace. Interesting. Could there be something to spark my interest there?

Right now there's no fire to be concerned about. But I wonder: Where does the fire go when it's burning? I mean, it doesn't come into the room. It seems to go up. One minute it's roaring and then it's gone. Where does it go? It seems to go up, but where? And why doesn't it ever come down? These are questions that deserve answering.

I look around to make sure I'm alone. You can never be too cautious. I mosey over to the fireplace. The screen is in place so I just look through it. It looks to be just a pile of ashes on and under the grate. No embers. No heat. But I can't see anything when I look to the top. Is there a hole there? I need to take a closer look.

I take my paw and try to pull the screen aside. It takes a bit of effort, but it eventually gives way. Tentatively I put my left paw into the fireplace, near the grate. Yes, I was right. No heat. A little sniff: It smells like....hmmm, ash and soot. And it looks a bit dirty so I'd better be careful. I don't want any tell-tale signs. Just a quick inspection and that should take care of it.

I move around the grate and look up. There appears to be a hole. And there seems to be a draft...the air is moving up. Maybe if I get a little closer...just up on the grate and...maybe if I reach up I'll be able to...Yes, yes, I can see it clearly now. There's a hole. And beyond that a vertical tunnel. So that's where the fire goes! But where does the tunnel lead? If I reach just a little further, maybe there's a ledge up there that I can climb onto. The tunnel is so dark, and I can't feel anything. A bigger stretch should do it. Just a little further....uh oh, oh no, oh no!

The next thing I know, I've landed back in the fireplace. Albeit on all fours, but the soot and ashes are flying...it seems like a sand storm. I don't move. Maybe no one heard the noise. Then I remember that no one is home to hear. And Cinders is out like a light so no problem there. But what type of mess have I created? Or maybe it's not a mess at all. I mean, once the ashes settle, it will look just the way I found it. I give it another minute and yes, the soot settles back on and under the grate. Just as it was. Slowly I move back through the open screen. Satisfied that all is as I found it, I move across the living room, back down the hallway to the den. Exhausted, I do a quick face cleanse, nestle on the couch and drift off.

✳✳✳

The key turning in the front door arouses me from my afternoon respite.

I'm home. Girls, I'm home. Where are you? Where…Oh my God, what happened here? Oh my God. The carpet. What happened?

I wake up alarmed. What could have happened? Did something happen while I napped? I didn't hear anything. What could have happened? What's going on?

I race out of the den and see that Cinders has already made it to the living room. She turns to me, and her eyes say it all. "Chloe, you're in real trouble now."

But...what did I do? I look up at Mom and see that...
Well, upset is a mild understatement.

Chloe Anne, what have you done? Look at the rug. Look at you. Oh my God, what a mess!

But what's the problem, I wonder. Everything in the living room looks in order. Except...what are those dark marks on the carpet? And what could they possibly have to do with me?

How am I going to get this out of the rug? How far does it go? The den? Oh great. Where else? You weren't on the couch, were you? Oh no, the couch, too? And you: You're filthy, Chloe Anne.

Filthy? *Moi?* Okay, enough of the disparagements. How bad can this be?

Chloe Anne

It won't matter how much you bathe yourself, Chloe Anne, you'll never get all that soot off of you. What were you doing in the fireplace? Why on earth would you go in there? Chloe Anne, you're a VERY bad girl. VERY BAD!

Muttering and sputtering, she goes into the bedroom and reappears in her most unattractive sweat clothes. What's the problem, I wonder? What's the big deal? She picks me up and holds me up in front of the mirror.

Cats can't see the same as humans, but I can tell that I'm one shade now, not two-toned as before. I look down and notice my tummy is dark. Oh, so, *that's* it.

Can I make amends? I think not. I don't even have a prize to present to her, something that will make her proud of my venture: No bird, no mouse, not even a spider. Just me. Turning in her arms to offer my best apology, I lift my face up and give her cheek a lick.

Young lady, don't even go there with me. The sweet stuff won't work right now. Okay, into the tub!

Oh noooooo!! The tub. Anything but the tub!!

***

Well, I survived the tub. And I survived Mom's wrath. She couldn't stay mad at me long. In fact, I don't think she got upset with me again until....

***

What's behind that door? Well, I know the washer and dryer, but why is the room verboten? Always a *Chloe, don't go in there,* and THE DOOR is shut. Or *Chloe, stay out,* and THE DOOR closes with Mom still in there. What's so special about that room? I've seen inside. Just two big, white boxes. Why no entrance privileges? Is she hiding something from me? Maybe this is where she stores the extra kitty treats. Perhaps the salmon ones? What could possible go wrong? Again, more questions that deserve answers.

It was late one Thursday afternoon. I remember it well because Thursday night is *"Ugly Betty/Grey's Anatomy"* night. Nothing keeps Mom from these two programs so I fully expected her home on time. As I was walking from the dry food dish in the kitchen, I noticed THE DOOR a bit ajar. Unusual. Mom is so careful about keeping it closed when she's not at home. I continue walking, but find myself stopping mid-step. My curiosity kicks in. What really is behind that door?

I look around. Cinders is nowhere in sight. It would be nice if she would stand guard. Just in case Mom gets home early. *Hmmm.* Should I? Do I dare? With only a momentary hesitation, I conclude: *But of course.*

I take my right paw and pull THE DOOR open. The lights are off in the room so I give my eyes some time to adjust. Yes, two big, white boxes. What else? Something tall and cylindrical. What could that be? I step cautiously around it. There looks to be a small blue flame behind a small compartment. Uh oh, I'd better not get any closer. Cats have memories, you know, and the fireplace fiasco will be forever imprinted on my mind. Besides, time is limited so I decide it best to examine only the washer and dryer.

They appear harmless enough to me. Side-by-side, one has a flat front surface, and the other has a closed door. I jump up on the latter, calculating (correctly) that its top surface would be flat and free of any encumberments.

There are wall shelves above the box, and they're filled with stuff. I'll leave them alone. Still, nothing unusual. Why doesn't she ever let me in then?

I move to the other box. Its door is on the top, and it's open! Well, this should shed some light on everything. What's inside? I peer in and find just a hole with a cylinder type object running down the center. What is this? Perhaps a little look-see wouldn't hurt. What's the harm in that? Short and sweet and that will be that.

I move into it slowly. Nothing. Well, I don't see what the big deal has been about. It's just an empty hole so I turn to jump out. Except...

The space is tight, and I can't maneuver the jump. Maybe if I stretch and reach the opening, I can pull myself up. Oops, slipped. Try again, Chlo, it can't be that difficult. And so I try again. Again and again until.... Oh no, oh no. My movements have jarred the lid and suddenly a slam, and I'm in the dark!

I stand on my hind legs and try to push it open. But it has me in its snare. It won't give an inch. How will I ever escape? And it's so dark. I'm trapped. How am I ever going to get out?

I start to meow, loudly. Maybe Cinders will hear me. I pause and wait. Nothing. Again and again I cry out for help, but she doesn't come. Oh my goodness, it's so dark in here and so cramped. I don't think I can breathe. I'll suffocate before anyone finds me. I'm so scared. Please help!!

***

I must have fallen asleep. I don't know how much time has passed. I feel weak. I know I'll be found sooner or later, but in enough time? I hear a distant noise. Is it the front door opening?

Force of Nature

I'm home. Girls, I'm home. Where are you? Hi, Cinder-Binders. How's my sweetie pie? Where's your sister? In the bedroom?

I cry out for help, but again, no one hears me. She must have gone into the bedroom. Isn't that what she does? The keys and purse are put on the console next to the door, and she goes to the bedroom. Shoes come off as she heads into the bathroom. Thirty seconds, forty, fifty...the toilet should flush. Yes, I hear it in the distance.

Chloe, where are you? Under the bed? No. Well, it's time for dinner. Come on out, wherever you are.

I'm trying to get out. I call to her, but to no avail. Even though I hear her in the kitchen, my cry is weak. She just can't hear me.

Chloe Anne

Cinders, what about some Gerber's veal tonight? I had such a great day. Why not a special treat?

Veal? I'm missing veal?

Chlo-bo, we're having veal. Where are you?

Back down the hallway I hear her move. I'm feeling so weak. I don't think I'm going to make it. What if I don't? What if I....? Will they hold a service for me? Perhaps a small soiree in my honor, celebrating my life. And will Mom put my obituary in the *New York Times*? "...our treasured Chloe Anne, a verdant and blooming girl, filled with grace, good humor and a better than average appetite for life and its plenty"....But no! Oh, I want to live, I want to live! Cinders, if you eat all the veal, I'll sit on you. Don't you dare eat all of it. Oh, Mom, please get me out of here!! Mom, I want my mom!

Chloe. Chloe! Where are you? Not under the bed, not in the closets. In the fireplace? No. Where are you hiding? Chloe, this isn't funny. Where are you?

I hear Mom's words, but importantly, I hear her tone. Alarmed. Frightened.

She's moving down the hallway again, in and out of rooms, thinking out loud. I meow to her: The laundry room! I'm here, I'm here. But I know my mew is faint.

Laundry room? I hear the door open and close, too quickly for me to.....*Oh no, did you get out again? But how could you have gotten out? Chloe, are you stuck behind the computer? The TV? Where are you hiding? Chlo-bo, no more games. Stop this. You're scaring me.*

Then, silence. Nothing but silence. Deafening. That's it. There's no hope. I'll never be saved. Resigned, I put my head down and await the inevitable. Until...

I hear pawing, light scratching at the door.

Cinders, I already checked there. She's not in there.

More pawing. Then, a full body thump. Ingenious. But, wait...what took her so long? Could it be? No, she isn't the selfish type. Did she do this on purpose? Did she wait until she finished her dinner? Oh, I don't care. I don't care. Mom, please pay attention to her. Open the door!

I hear the laundry door open one more time.

See, sweetie, she's not here. There's no place she can hide in here. Unless she...no. The lids are all shut.

I hear the dryer door open and shut. Oh, please, please. Open this one next. And then, blinding light!

Oh my God, Chloe. How did you get in here? Are you okay? Oh, my little Chlo-bo, are you okay? Come here. Let's get you out of there. Oh my Chlo-bo, I was so scared. Are you okay? How did my little adventurer get in there? What happened? Thank goodness for Cinders insisting I check again.

She pulls me up and carries me to the couch. No broken bones, just a bruised ego in need of repair. So lots of cuddling and kisses ensue. But not before I notice the food plate licked clean, and Cinders sitting, calmly cleaning her face. She glances at me, a bemused look on her face, and her eyes say it all: "It's time for you to clean up your act, sis."

I may be frazzled, but considering that I spent the afternoon trapped in a washing machine, I can certainly appreciate her humor. But is there some truth in what she's thinking? Have I pushed my limits? I know I'm only promised nine lives. Perhaps there's a lesson to be learned from this, but what it is I can't think of at the moment. All I know is that I owe her big time. I only hope I can repay her while we both still have our nine lives.

Chapter Ten

*   *   *   *   *

Sharing the Bed

I mentioned earlier the nuances of sleeping without speaking directly about sleep itself. Where does sleeping, you may wonder, fall within all the subsets? Or does it? I'm glad you asked.

There's (1) sleeping and then there's (2) SLEEPING. We're talking #2 now. Sleeping is restricted to the night hours, generally between 11 p.m. and 6 a.m. Now, some cats like to be up and about during that time, but not us. We're quite civilized, perhaps excessively so even for felines, and appreciate every restful moment afforded to us.

Night sleeping is the deepest slumber so it requires the greatest preparation. We start by having a long drink of water. Mom always keeps a dish in the bedroom, usually tap water but sometimes, just sometimes, she'll take a bottle of Evian that she hasn't finished and fills our dish with it. It may not sound like much to others but bottled water definitely has a crisper, cleaner taste than straight out of the tap.

Then, up onto the bed to commence our evening body wash. We start with extensive bathing. After all, we share the bed with Mom so even if the sheets aren't freshly laundered, we like to believe we are. Top to bottom, all the nooks and crannies. This takes a bit of time but it works out okay because Mom is usually puttering around, doing her own pre-bed prep. When she turns off the lights in the living room and makes one last check to ensure she turned off the oven and stove, and turns on the house alarm, we each take a quick turn in the litter box. No need to have a deep sleep interrupted, if you know what I mean.

Back onto the bed, we wait expectantly for her. And finally, FINALLY, she makes it to bed.

Come on, girls. Time for bed. Who wants a pet? Who wants to play laser light?

I want the former, something calm and soothing before dropping off. But Cinders? For a fairly quiet girl, she suddenly starts to talk, almost chirps. She gets quite excited and jumps off the bed, all the while looking with great anticipation at Mom. Eyes bright, her raccoon tail all filled out, you'd think the world had stood still just for her. Well, maybe it did because Mom opens the bedside table drawer and pulls out "THE LASER LIGHT." The chirping turns into a low meow and you can see her body tighten to attention, like a steel spring, ready to move to action. Mom turns on the flashlight, the red laser light shines on the floor, and Cinders goes ballistic.

She jumps to it, following it wherever Mom moves it. Across the room, down the hall, up the chair. Nothing stops her, even when it's shined on the wall. Jumping, hurling herself against it. The huntress in her comes out in all her glory. She's the lioness that knows no bounds. I stare in fascination. I can never get enough of the show. It's as if her alter ego comes to the fore, and nothing can hold it back. And then, when you think she's had enough, for she sits herself sphinx-like squarely on the floor near the bed (really one of her most attractive poses if I say so myself), you realize it's only intermission.

Act II commences with short movements of the laser, barely six inches apart. The objective, I've learned, is for Cinders to trap the light all while maintaining her position. It takes great coordination and above all else, focus. And she is the Mistress of Focus. Then, one more intermission and the finale: The light is shined to the end of the hall. She sprints to follow it, knowing that at any moment it could reverse its direction. Does it? And what about her turn radius? Will she be able to make the 180° without hitting the furniture? Can she make it back up the hall to the bedroom, stopping on a dime without crashing into the bedside table? Will she? Can she? Does she? The crescendo is deafening. Yes, yes, she does!!!

And then, oh my God, the audience (Mom) calls for an ovation. *More, sweetie? Come on up.*

Is she up to it? Yes, she is!!! The crowd (Mom and I) cheer. Up onto the bed, taking short sprints across the coverlet as the red light starts and stops. Here and there, up and down. She never loses her focus, never loses ground. And then, in that proverbial blink of an eye...the light is off!!! I can't believe it. I'm stunned. But Cinders, she takes it in stride. After all, she's the Mistress of Focus, and the light will return another evening, yet again to challenge her skills and dexterity. She quietly turns and moves to the foot of the bed. Gracefully she sits and repeats her evening bath. No fur out of place, not even breaking a sweat.

Well, I'm exhausted at this point and need a cuddle. That took a lot of energy out of me. I watch as Mom puts the flashlight back in the drawer and picks up either her *New York Times* crossword puzzle or whatever book she's reading at the moment. I move to her left side and place myself firmly against her hip with my head nuzzling into her waist.

Hi, sweet girl? How's my Chlo-bo? Time for a little love, huh, sweetie-pie?

Some serious petting takes place, all while she's either completing 4-Down or 27-Across. Then it's lights off, and we just settle in for the night.

It's a queen size bed...just perfect for three. And it's a nice arrangement, comfortable and cozy. One we never thought would change. Until....

Chapter Eleven

* * * * *

A Hiss is Just a Hiss

His name is Cortes. *Cortes.* Not Antonio. Not Placido. But Cortes. Not even with a "z" but with an "s."

I can't believe Mom would do this to us. She must be losing her mind. It happened two weeks ago, and Cinders and I are still reeling.

***

Sunday. Mom's *"NY Times"* Day. Usually a "sleep-in-I-don't-have-to-work-please-girls-fend-for-yourselves" day. Mom never truly lets us fend for ourselves, but you get the picture.

As I hear it, the following transpired: Out she went to meet Rebekah, a friend she met through her ballroom dancing activities. Rebekah is a very peppy, optimistic sort. Lots of energy. Most important, however, is that she is the proud mom of two cats, Beelzebub and Fancy Pants. Very feline-friendly.

So in the course of their wanderings, they came upon one of those weekend cat adoptions. You know, when an organization sets up shop in front of a pet store with several cages housing homeless kittens and cats. I heard about these types of activities during my time in the Big House, and I must admit, it really is a commendable idea.

It all sounds rather suspect to me...probably Mom was set up...but the bottom line is this: Mom came home late that afternoon, *sans chat*. At least literally speaking. First to the bathroom, then checking her phone messages. One call she returned gave the two of us the head's up.

Chloe Anne

Jean, you wouldn't believe what happened today. Rebekah and I were at the mall. There was a cat adoption going on, and the cutest little Persian was available…cameo colored, topaz eyes…name is Cortes…I don't really need another cat. Three might be quite a handful…No, I didn't make a commitment. I'm just thinking about it. His owner died. He doesn't have anyplace to go…I'm not sure how the girls will take it. You think I should? You and Rebekah. I don't get it. Why the interest in my getting another one?

Now, Mom knows that not much gets past Cinders and me, and the fact that we were dozing in the bedroom while the two of them spoke on the phone…Three feet away from us…Hello?!?! Rather than bolt, become hysterical, act out, we chose to wait and see. Would she tell us anything?

We waited. Nothing more was said about this "Cortes" so our waiting continued.

***

Dinnertime approached, and the two of us were surprised with a little broiled salmon treat. Something clearly was up. Now of course, that didn't keep us from licking the dish to a shine. But we didn't just fall off the turnip truck, if you know what I mean.

After watching *Ebert & Roeper* and *Sixty Minutes*, the television was turned off, and we heard,

Girls, come here. We need to talk.

Well, lest I bore you with most of the details that you've already heard, Mom broke the news to us: She was thinking of adopting this cat. And we knew she was just thinking. Nothing decided, just yet. She's pretty thorough when it comes to making decisions. Not that we had a vote, mind you. But we knew that she always looked at all sides of an issue before making a decision. And most certainly one as important as this one would involve a lot of "do I's or don't I's?" Probably a good two weeks of deliberation by my count. Plenty of time to influence her otherwise. What were Aunt Jean and Rebekah thinking, anyway?

***

So much for the two week window. The following Wednesday evening, upon her return from work, Mom checked her phone messages. One was from that shelter about Cortes: Is Mom still interested?

She picked up the phone and dialed.

Jean, they called, and Cortes is still available…Yeah…Yeah. He is such a sweet kitty…They told me that the woman's son had left him outside to fend for himself, and the neighbor found him pawing at the front door, trying to get back inside.

This was new information. I was all ears.

Didn't he know the cat is declawed? The cat has probably never been outside. Who would do that? Well, I'm leaning towards it. He doesn't have a home, and I keep seeing his face. It would be an adjustment, but I'm sure the girls would be fine with it...

Mom sat on the bed, not moving. Just kind of staring at the wall, with an occasional mutter to no one in particular: *How cold. I just can't believe it. Who would do that to a defenseless animal?*

I moved up on the bed and nestled against her hip. I must say that my previous owners NEVER put me outside and closed the door. The anguish in Mom's voice was palpable. Absentmindedly she petted my head.

What should I do, Chlo? There's something about this little guy that is so special? Remember when you and I first met? I looked at you and just knew. I mean, it's not really the same, but...well, you understand. I just can't get his little face out of my mind.

My thoughts went back to that time in the Big House, the day we first met.

I wanted to remind her that one difference was that she had been actively looking for a companion for Cinders. She wasn't casually out with a friend, window shopping. There was an immediate *simpatico* between us, and we both knew it was special.

I looked up at her and pushed my head into her hand. I knew what direction the wind was blowing. Was I happy about it? I don't think so. But I know there are times we all have to rise above our petty concerns. Take the high road, so to speak. Mom must have felt something very special about this Cortes to make such a drastic change to our family unit. It would be a challenge, but the Big House taught me all about challenges.

Mom looked down and softly scratched my chin.

I know this will be an adjustment for us all, Chlo, but I want him to come live with us. There's always enough love to go around. Can I count on you, Chlo? I thought so. That's my good girl. Come on. Let's go tell Cinders.

***

Two weeks later Mom came through the door with a cat carrier. I recognized it from when she first brought me home. Into the den, closing the door behind her.

We both knew the drill and waited. And waited. And waited. Eventually Mom came out and closed the door behind her.

C'mon, girls. Let's have dinner.

Cinders and I looked at each other. Hmmm. Well, okay. We'll just follow her lead. Up and off to the kitchen. She quickly pulled together a mix of wet and dry and placed our dishes on the floor. As she started to chop vegetables for her salad, we heard the events of the afternoon and the evening's schedule.

He's a little scared, girls. Not because of his bath…in fact, he seemed to really enjoy it….particularly the hair blower…but he wasn't thrilled about seeing the vet. All the poking and prodding got him upset. He seems to be a delicate little guy. So I'm going to spend some more time with him and then the two of you can visit.

And with chopped salad and a small dish of dry cat food in hand, she went back to the den, closing the door behind her.

My antennae were up, albeit *pink* flags not red. I can't say why. I wonder if Cinders felt like this when I first came home? I looked over and saw her calming munching on supper. Ever poised, ever serene. No clue to her thoughts. Well, best to put my questions and doubts on hold. Dinner was waiting.

✳✳✳

About thirty minutes later, the den door reopened. The two of us were in the living room and lest we (I?) appear anxious, we took our time moving down the hall to the den. Turning into the room, we saw Mom on the couch with what can only be described as a cameo-caramel cotton ball ensconced on her lap. I heard a short hiss from Cinders, but I just stared. Cat? *Cat?*

Let me assure you he certainly didn't look like any cat I had ever seen, and my unfortunate incarceration had allowed me time to see many a breed come and go. His face? Round with full cheeks. His eyes were like topaz saucers. Ears small and pointed, set far apart. His nose? Oh my God, maybe some might describe it as short and broad, but to me it just looked squished flat up against his face. Small mouth, seemingly in a frown. Looked more like an owl than a cat, if I say so myself.

But other than the initial shock, he looked harmless enough. And small! He couldn't have been more than six pounds underneath all that fur. And gosh, what fur. I thought mine was long, but his was so dense and full. Did he use a conditioner? Maybe Pantene. But wait, that's not the point. Whatever doubts I may have had disappeared. Okay, so he was already on Mom's lap and seemed content to never move. I could set him straight on that soon enough. But for now I think this might...

Was I going to say "work"? After hearing Mom's soft, *C'mon, girls, time for introductions,* let's just say something hit the proverbial fan. Cinders sat to my left, and I heard a low growl. What? Then, a series of hisses. Her body movements said it all: It's time to set the boundaries. She was on a roll. There was no holding her back. Her tail looked to be the size of an engorged hose. She started to move forward, then stopped. The hissing continued in short spurts, and Cortes returned in-kind. Back and forth, back and forth. To and fro, to and fro—like Nadal and Federer at the French Open.

Stop it, Mom interjected, with no effect. What was she thinking? Did she really think her words would have any impact?

Cortes maintained his position on Mom's lap. Pretty smart cookie, I thought, above the fray, in the dominant position. And the way he raised his fur on his back and tail...he looked massive! So male! More hissing, more posturing. My, I love a man who's willing to take a stand, who won't back down. An aphrodisiac if ever there was one. I could watch him for....

Wait! What am I thinking? Have I lost my mind? This is crazy. He just walked in the door. This is *our* home! Enough already. Señor Cortes, you'll be welcomed but on our terms...Señor? Persian? What isn't right with this picture?...We know you've had a rough time, but you can't just waltz in here (Hmmm, I wonder if he can rumba?) and expect an easy go of it.

Again, Mom tried to diffuse the situation: *Stop it, you two!*

You two? Not anymore. You have more than one feline to contend with, Señor Cortes. Right now Cinders needs my support. She shouldn't carry this burden alone. It's payback time. She needs to know that I have her back and her wing-cat won't let her down. If Tom Cruise can do it, so can I! It can't be so very hard. Swept up in the passion of the moment, my head high, my teeth bared, I opened my mouth and......

.........nothing.

Both heads turned. The silence was deafening. Staring. Mouths gaping, two set of eyes focused on me.

I opened my mouth again and, again......

.........nothing.

Oh my God! How embarrassing! How exposed I felt! Like Wonder Woman without her supernatural power or Xena the Warrior Princess without her Herculean strength. I couldn't hide it anymore. The shame I had lived with all these years. My secret was out:

I DON'T KNOW HOW TO HISS!!!

Cortes squirmed off Mom's lap and down to the carpet. A circle formed, albeit more of a triangle of them versus me. Staring. Curious. Surprised expressions on their faces. And then. And then the expressions changed.

Cinders' eyes questioning: "Why didn't you tell me? You could have told me."

And Cortes, seemingly speechless, but not really: "I've never known a cat who couldn't hiss. But that doesn't matter to me. I just want to look at you. You're sooooo beautiful."

My look to Cinders was apologetic, but she paid no heed. She was all appreciation and pride—for my being her wing-cat, regardless of the pain it must have evoked. She knew she could always count on me.

And to Cortes, a flattered but indulgent smile. After all, he *is* a man, albeit younger. He certainly came around quite easily. Perhaps a bit wet behind the ears? No matter. What did Miss Jean Brodie say about girls at impressionable ages? Well, I may be taking more than my share of literary license, but with a few months' time maybe I'll have him...?

Three sets of expectant eyes shifted to Mom. *Are you three finished now? A little peace and quiet so I can watch Law & Order? Then it's time for bed.*

***

Bed? You may be wondering how we ended up sharing the bed, now with three cats instead of two. It seems Cortes caught on quite quickly...well, after a little feminine feline pushing and prodding. After one rotation and two gentle kneads, he was on Mom's pillow, above and nestled into her head. It seems we have the situation...or better said, *Mom*...covered.

Chapter Twelve

* * * * *

Oscar was Right: True friends stab you in the front.

I 'd like to say that I never knew who betrayed me, but that would be a lie. It was Aunt Jean. She didn't have to say anything. Mom never had to know. But no, Aunt Jean had to make a big *meshugas* about it. She made it sound like a crime had been committed. And she didn't waste anytime telling Mom. But was it fact or fiction? You be the judge.

***

It was evening, and I noticed that the suitcase was out again. Empty, but the three of us knew the routine: It would be filled with clothes that night, and the next morning Mom would be traveling. Where to *this* time? *Maine.*

Her business trips never fazed us. They usually lasted only a couple of days, and then she'd be home again. Although Uncle Rodney usually came to stay with us, recently Aunt Jean had been helping Mom out. She never stayed overnight like Uncle Rodney. Rather, she'd come in the morning and evening just to feed us. She always made time to play and socialize with us, but, quite frankly, we knew that her arrival meant "food" so we weren't in the mood to make small talk. In hindsight, I think we were rude to her and hurt her feelings. Maybe that's why she, you'll pardon the expression, let the cat out of the bag.

Anyway, this time the trip was not for business, but rather a vacation. And not just *any* vacation: Mom would be gone for *three weeks*! I can't imagine why she would want to be away for so long, but it was all set, so who were *we* to argue? She left, the days went by, and nothing of any consequence occurred. Well, not really...

***

The morning before Mom's return, I noticed Cinders and Cortes sitting on the living room couch, cleaning each other. Even though we all got along, having three cats in the family had changed the dynamics a bit. At first, Cortes had a crush on me. I wasn't interested in him in that sort of way, but sometimes a little adoration can really lift a girl's spirit. Not that I worry about my ego, but that whole episode with the hissing really threw me off balance. I was feeling a little self-conscious, and he seemed to like me so I thought a little extra attention might do the trick.

Well, I had no idea of the depth of his attraction, and the next thing I knew he was pretty much glued to my hip. Usually when men come to visit, they leave after a certain amount of time. But Cortes was here ALL THE TIME. Wanting to spend time with me, wanting to watch my adventures, wanting to share meals with me...wanting to sleep with me! I mean, ALL THE TIME.

I was flattered that he took such a liking to me, but I couldn't let it continue. So I dropped him. Perhaps a callous disregard for his affections, but I didn't know what else to do.

The next thing I knew, he and Cinders were quite chummy. At first it didn't faze me because I understand… and I mean no disrespect to Cinders…but men will be men. They don't mourn; they replace. Usually I wasn't bothered by it because Mom was there. But with her away and for so long, I really felt a little lonely.

I jumped up on the coffee table, just to get their attention. I thought I could land easily without inflicting any damage. I know I'm a big girl, but I'm very agile. But my tail and backside inadvertently hit the vase. The next thing I knew, everything went flying. I looked around: Cinders and Cortes were no longer in sight. What to do? What to do? Well, nothing broke. But Aunt Jean? She notices everything. And she'll be here soon to feed us. I'll just have to distract her. That's it. She's been asking to play with us since Mom left. I'll just divert her attention. And then Mom will be back tomorrow, and everything will be fine. Okay, problem solved!

***

I heard the key in the door. Yea! Time for breakfast. Aunt Jean couldn't have gotten here soon enough. I'm starving!

Hi you three! Time to eat. What shall we have today?... What? Who's that rubbing my leg. Chloe Anne, aren't you being a sweetheart. What's going on? Why are you playing nice? This isn't like you.

Playing nice? I'm always nice.

She lifted me up until we were face-to-face. *Now, you know I love this attention, but it seems a little too much of a good thing. Particularly from you. Something's up, Chloe Anne. What's going on?*

Chloe Anne

I looked back at her, eyes wide in amazement: It's just that I'm so glad you're here to take care of us. I love you so much, Aunt Jean. Could you stay a little longer today and play?

Something isn't right, Ms. Chlo. You're up to something.

She put me down and finished getting our food ready. Cinders and Cortes came in and quietly started eating. I was already at my bowl, and watched her as I munched. Uh oh, something's not working. Usually she puts our dishes down and waits in the den until we're done. But this time, she left the kitchen and started looking around. Dare I admit this? My appetite was waning. Would she notice? Silly question.

Oh no, what happened here? Chloe? Cinders? Cortes? Who did this?

Cortes and Cinders kept eating their food, ignoring her call. Well, what did they have to worry about anyway? I decided it best to respond and followed her to the living room. There I watched as she fussed and muttered. *Okay, the vase isn't broken...good...water all over...irises and daffodils...have to stop the water from staining the wood. Chloe! How did this happen?*

Me? Maybe it was Cinders. Maybe it was Cortes.

She picked me up and held me close to the table and dripping water. *Did you do this? Why would you do this?*

Me? Why me?

She put me down and started wiping up the water. *Wait until your mom hears about this.*

Mom? Why Mom? Can't this just be between you and me? Why bring her into this? Aunt Jean just looked at me as though I had committed a heinous crime. Before I knew it, I was on her lap.

Chloe, maybe it was Cortes or Cinders. But I highly doubt it. Remember the fireplace?

That was a safety precaution. I was just making sure the fire had an escape route.

Or scratching apart the entire underside of the box spring?

Aunt Jean, it's one of my hiding places.

Or what about your Mom's suitcase?

But that was really an accident!! Aunt Jean, I always sleep in her suitcase before she goes away. I have to be sure she'll remember me and return. I couldn't help it that I drank too much water before going to sleep that time. It was an accident!!

Chloe, I know about your mischievous side. Your mom always talks about it. You're always at excitement's cutting edge, but sometimes you have to be a little more careful. I know how passionate you are about life, that you're not afraid of taking risks. But Mom will have to be told about this.

I nuzzled up against her, purring with all my might. What could I do to change her mind?

Sometimes it's best just to be honest, Chloe Anne.

You're right, Aunt Jean, in this case, honesty is definitely the best policy (Thank goodness she didn't notice the linen closet. Or litter box. Then I'd *really* be in trouble!).

Chapter Thirteen

* * * * *

A Home by Any Other Name

Indian summer. Even though we're in Northern California, the leaves start to turn ever so slightly. And while the air is still warm, you can smell the tang of autumn coming. Ah, autumn.

But I'm sensing something more than just leaves in the air this September. We all are. It doesn't seem to phase Cinders much because she's very good rolling with the punches. But Cortes has only been here a short time, and he seems jittery and agitated. He keeps giving me questioning glances, but all I can do is offer a reassuring shrug: I don't know what's going on either. But if there is something, we'll learn soon enough. Mom won't keep us in the dark. Don't worry.

Yet I must admit, even I'm beginning to wonder. Mom's cleaning out the closets: Bags of items are either being donated or thrown out. And she's been on the phone a lot. Not only with the usual suspects...Aunt Jean, Uncle Rodney, Aunt Sunny...but to a woman named Carolyn. We've heard phrases like...closing costs, property appraisal, interest rates....but none of it makes sense to us. And then, the most mysterious one of all: *Let's show it like a museum. I'll leave a piece of furniture and artwork in each room.* What's going on? Is Mom changing careers? Is she going to be a museum curator? Now we're truly perplexed.

✱✱✱

But not for long. A week passes, and the three of us notice that the bags of trash and donations have been replaced by boxes. And to my eye, they appear to be moving boxes! I only say this because I remember...oh, how I remember! It's all coming back to me: all the flutter, packing, boxing, tossing things out. Uh oh, could this mean Mom's moving?? And if so, will that mean....???

I don't let Cinders or Cortes know of my concerns. They've experienced their own unique upheavals:

Cinders first lost her mom, Grandma Peggy, and then she had to fly on an airplane to live with Mom. The roar of the takeoff and landing, being in a cage in a cargo hold: Scary, very scary.

And Cortes: Thinking of his being shut out of his house after his first mom died still makes me shudder. And I know about being kept in a cage, waiting to be adopted. But I'm a lot stronger than he is. Mom was right: He's a sensitive little guy. Any changes at this point would really upset him.

I think it best I not say anything. After all, I could be wrong, and I wouldn't want them unnecessarily upset. It's best to wait and see.

So I keep my fears to myself, and the three of us continue to exchange questioning glances. But to no avail. None of us knows anything. And then....

Mom gathers us all in the den, turns off the TV and closes the door. Uh oh, she wants our undivided attention, no escape route available to any of us. And she doesn't mince words. She cuts straight to the chase.

Force of Nature

Okay, here's the poop. We're moving!

We freeze and stare. No noise is uttered. I think to myself: Be strong. Be strong for Cinders and Cortes. I look to my right.

Cinders: Her face shows nothing. Just waiting. She knows there's probably more to this than Mom is saying at the moment. She waits. It will all come out soon enough.

Cortes: Total bewilderment. His eyes grew rounder with every second. I didn't think they could get any larger than they already were. But I just got here, they said beseechingly. Where are we going?

Me: For appearances sake, I'm calm. But the mini-drama in my head is far from it. I need some air. I keep up my outward appearance, trying to be as nonchalant as possible and move to the door. Curiously, Mom doesn't hesitate and lets me out. I wonder why? I look quickly over my shoulder and give Cortes a look of encouragement: There's nothing to worry about. Just stay with her, and she'll answer all of your questions. I just need to use the litter box. I'll be back.

Litter box, my eye. I head straight to the bed and crawl under. My breathing is rapid, and I'm dizzy. I know what's happening. She let me out of the room because she's telling them privately: *The three of us are moving, but Chloe will have to stay behind. All of her adventures are too much for the household, too disruptive. But don't worry, she'll be just fine. The SPCA will find a home that is better equipped to handle her passion for excitement.*

I guess this wasn't the real thing after all. Maybe if I sleep, I'll wake up and find this is all just a horrible dream. That's what I'll do. I'll sleep. And when I wake up, it will all be gone, and I won't need to be frightened anymore. I hear Mom talking to Cinders and Cortes and allow myself to drift off. It's a bad dream, just a bad dream.

✳✳✳

Chloe, Chloe, wake up. Why are you hiding under the bed? Come on out. You slept through dinner, sweetie pie. Don't you feel well?

I open an eye and see Mom's face, peering under the bed. She looks concerned, and then I remember what was said earlier. I close my eye. Please leave me alone. I can't talk right now.

Chloe, are you sick? Come here. Let me hold you.

I don't know how to tell her that she's the reason I feel ill. But perhaps it best not to drag it out any longer. I have to face the music sooner or later. So with great trepidation and reluctance, I come out from under the bed and let her pick me up.

Sweetie, let's go sit in the den. I've already talked to Cinders and Cortes, and they understand everything about the move. I wanted to talk to you privately, to explain it all to you, but you never came back in the room.

I was right. I knew it. As we head into the den, I glance down and see the other two. Surprisingly they are exceptionally calm. I don't understand. Doesn't it bother them that I'm being given away?

Mom closes the door, and we sit on the couch. I'm in Step One, facing her and again I hear:

We're moving…

I can't help it. Just hearing the words brings on a spasm. My heart starts to palpitate, my neck fur stands on end, panting is next. Oh, no, a major anxiety attack. I haven't had one of these in ages. I'd been feeling so safe and secure. What can I do? I try to focus, to listen to her words.

…It's a big house…

Big House? Oh my God, I'm going back to jail. You are getting rid of me. Please don't get rid of me. I won't take any more adventures. I'll be on my best behavior.

Please don't abandon me. My breathing is rapid, I'm dizzy and feeling faint.

...The rooms are large so you won't feel cramped...

Not feel cramped? You've never been in one of those cells. They're claustrophobic. Oh Mom, I'm so sorry...for whatever I've done. Please give me another chance. I'll make it up to you. I'll be good. I promise.

So, what do you think, Chlo-bo? Wouldn't you like a bigger house? With a view of the water?

A view of the water? Oh my God, I'm being sent to Alcatraz. You weren't supposed to take my comment about Burt literally!

Now, Chloe Anne. This move means I'll be closer to work. And that means I'll be home more. Would you like that? No more being scared that I won't come home to you. No more worries that I'll travel away, and leave you behind.

You mean, we're....? Can it be true? Do you...Do you really mean....??

Did you think I didn't understand? You're my big, beautiful girl. I couldn't live anywhere without you. Why, I wouldn't live anywhere without you!

I can't believe my ears. We're moving! Together! As a family! And there's *water?* I tilt my head, and the *kvelling* starts anew.

Hmmm, is that *fish* I smell...?